After the Storm

After the Storm

Nate Matthew's Journey
Toward Recovery

M-A Aden

To order additional copies of this book, contact:
Xlibris Corporation
1-888-795-4274
www.Xlibris.com
Orders@Xlibris.com
44486

For the One who makes me Real.

THE STORM

It was too easy to hear the desperate cries of the men housed on the floor below. "Get us out of here!" "You can't just leave us. We are going to drown!" "Please, help us . . . Help us! . . . Please, please help . . ."

"Why don't they get them out of there?" Hank asked his fellow inmates who were huddled there, also locked in their prison dormitory area, just one floor above. "Are they going to let them drown? What's happening?"

"They can't let them out," replied Nate Matthews. "The electrical controls that lock all the cells in the building are in the basement. If the second floor is flooding, the basement is already under. Everything is shorted out. If we want to live, we are going to have to break out of here." He was already looking around the room for ways to escape the situation.

Escaping prison was not something that Nate had ever considered while serving his five-year sentence for a series of drug related charges, the most serious of which was *Possession With Intent to Distribute Cocaine.*

Nate considered himself to be one of the lucky ones in addiction—someone who had entered recovery before his addiction cost him his life or his sanity. It was costing him his freedom, five years of his life away from his wife and son.

At the time of his arrest, Nate had surrendered his life to his Higher Power, who for Nate was Jesus Christ. He had trusted Him to lead him thru the journey of his sobriety, to present him with any lesson or suffering that would make him stronger and more able to leave prison free of his active addiction as well as his incarceration. Nate had been very serious when he had told God that he was "sick and tired of being sick and tired" of his life and his way of living. His Higher Power had given him hope and led him this far and Nate prayed for guidance even now as he looked for a way to escape.

Nate spoke to the others. "Let's see if we can jar this bed loose," he directed. Ten men familiar with the weight bench put all their strength and surging adrenaline into the act. The bed, which was bolted to the floor, began to move slightly. The men continued rocking the metal frame until they were able to break it loose.

The pieces of the frame came loose and each man took a part and moved toward the glassed-in overlook where guards had observed inmates in the living area of the prison. The glass was thick, designed for safety. Nate and the others pounded the glass as they heard the last of the cries from the floor below.

When the glass finally began to give and pieces of the remaining were torn hurriedly away allowing the inmates to crawl through to the overlook area, Nate thought again how unbelievable it seemed to him to be breaking out of prison. He looked back at the room that had been his home for the last months. As he followed the last man through the opening in the glass, he realized that he had never believed that anything could make him break the law again, but then he had not counted on a hurricane named Katrina . . .

CHAPTER 1

Once they were out of the locked dormitory and standing on the desktop in the observation room, the ten inmates considered their next option. It had to be up. With one of the smaller men standing on the shoulders of one of the larger, they were able to lift the tiles in the ceiling and pull themselves one by one into a similar observation area on the floor above. Now the men who were banded together in their fight for survival were able to force open the door to the outside hallway.

Once in the hallway, they started to run toward the stairs at the end of the unit. A former athlete, Nate reached the stairwell first and started taking the steps leading to the landing two or three at a time. When he reached the open space, he saw the barrel of the assault rifle before he heard the voice of the guard.

"Stop right where you are," the guard said. He, and a second guard, had rifles aimed, ready to stop the progress of the men who did not heed their command. Nate quickly recognized how desperate even the guards were and how easy it would have been to rid themselves of the responsibility of these ten prisoners. His hands went up in the universal gesture of surrender. The other prisoners mimicked his stance.

"Please," Nate gasped, out of breath from the exertion, "we are just trying to live, not escape. We have all got to get out of here or we are going to drown. What has happened out there?"

The inmates had long since lost radio contact with the outside world and even when they pooled batteries from their own radios and tape players, they had been unable to follow reports from the outside. The second guard spoke, "The levee broke. Water is flooding the whole city!"

It seemed impossible. Nate had lived in New Orleans all his life, always feeling safe from the Mississippi River. The river had been a friend to the area, providing the opportunity for the bulk of its commerce and defining the area as a thing of beauty, a tourist attraction to the entire world. Could it be possible that the Mississippi itself had turned against them?

"Then we've got to go," Nate said quickly. "We are in one of the lowest places in this ward." The guard motioned with the rifle and the inmates went ahead of the two guards toward the roof of the building.

The roof had been easier to access since the guards had master keys. The day and a half on the roof had been far better than the two on the bridge that had followed. On the roof, the guards had finally realized that the men in their charge were not looking to escape, but to survive. They were prisoners, but prisoners with trustee status. These were men who had benefitted from incarceration, men who had used their time in the department of corrections to examine their errors in thinking that had brought them to a life of crime.

Nate was not the only man among them who had experienced the Spiritual Awakening that is essential to the 12-Step recovery program he practiced. He had almost a year and a half of sobriety and was hoping to return to his family, still sober, after many years of difficult living as an addict in the streets of New Orleans. This rooftop experience was only a shadow of the hardships to come.

The men were finally evacuated from the rooftop to an inaccessible bridge on interstate ten. It had been a Wildlife and Fisheries agent who had come for them in a boat, loading all the men and the two guards into the small vessel for the trip to the bridge. At the bridge, the group had joined almost one hundred fifty other prisoners, guarded by eight men, again with assault rifles.

The custody there had been more difficult. It had to be. The prisoners were Louisiana men, for the most part. Men, who as boys, had learned to swim in the bayous of the Louisiana swamps. Slipping into the flood waters and avoiding years of incarceration seemed like a good option for some. Nate had no intention of making such an error in judgment. He complied with every order, sitting cross-legged in handcuffs for the terrible hours of the wait for further evacuation. He wanted to see his wife and son again, see them as a free man. He continued to trust God to protect and guide him and bring him safely home.

Near the end of the second day on the bridge, help had arrived in the form of the Department of Corrections. Scaffolding was lowered to the span of the highway beneath the bridge, connecting two levels of highway. Men grown weak from days without food and water, climbed steadily downward, lowering themselves to the highway below. They were met there with more guards, more assault rifles and handcuffs for the trip to the center that would process prisoners to new housing.

The stench of the waters and the odors on the bus were deplorable, but no one cared. Nate felt dazed and weak, but hopeful. He looked out onto the flooded city—it still rained! As the bus carrying Nate and the others pulled into the prison processing center, it was followed by eight others of equal size. Already, unkempt men were standing in long lines, waiting.

There were not enough guards and the ones there were weak from the same exhaustion and lack of food that the inmates had suffered. Nate looked up at the open yard of the huge prison facility. It was then that it became clear to him that he was going to be one of many, perhaps four thousand, who would be given a blanket and a jacket and told to continue inside into the fenced area.

He could not believe it! The time he had spent in prison made him aware of the danger in the yard. Rival gangs, murderers, rapists, offenders of all types were loose in the large fenced area, being guarded from a distance by men with weapons. A lot could happen before anyone was even aware there was danger.

Nate received his jacket and blanket and looked about for a place to rest. It was raining and there was no protection from the elements. He recognized a group of four others who were preparing to sleep in an area near the fence. Nate joined them.

He wondered how the prison officials would even attempt to feed this group. He had his answer pretty quickly when he heard a commotion near the opposing fence. Supply guards were throwing food over the fence to those incarcerated on the inside. It was too dangerous for anyone to enter the yard.

Nate skipped even trying for a meal and went instead to stand in one of the long lines waiting to drink water from one of two hoses that ran freely. Night came. Huddled, cold and wet, underneath his blanket, Nate tried not to hear the agonies of those who were assaulted for jackets, blankets, or hoarded food.

Physically, Nate was unharmed that night. He was, he would always believe, protected once again by the God who now ruled his life. Late the next day, he was directed to another bus to be carried to the airport. He was bound for a federal facility in Texas.

On board the plane that was filled with guards and other prisoners, Nate settled in. As the plane lifted into the air, Nate was able to look down on his native Louisiana. As he saw the flood waters still moving to cover familiar ground, he thought of his own life and the flood of changes he had experienced since finally surrendering. He was reminded of his earnest prayer, spoken only to God in the back of the police car at the time of his arrest. "I give up," Nate had prayed. "I've made an absolute mess of my life. I have tried, but I cannot quit the drugs. Do whatever you need to do to me, Father. Take my life . . . it is Yours!"

Three weeks after sentencing, almost forty days after his prayer of surrender, Nate had been placed in the first of two alcohol and drug treatment programs for offenders with drug and alcohol histories. He was on his way to learning to live sober.

CHAPTER 2

Nathan Matthews poured a tall glass of milk and replaced the carton into the refrigerator door. He lifted his LSU baseball cap and shook his head, causing his thick, dark hair to almost hide his green eyes. As he shut the door, he felt his mother watching him. "What?" he asked her directly, because he knew that *look* from his mother meant that they were about to have a serious discussion about something.

Nathan wondered if he were in trouble and thought about school. The year was almost over and he would be going into high school next year. He could think of nothing that would disturb his mother. His grades and behavior were good, in fact his coach had complimented him and two other guys on being leaders by continuing to make the honor roll even with so many games and practices. Nathan knew he had to have good grades as well as be an exceptional athlete in order to live his dream, the dream of wearing a Tiger uniform and playing sports for Louisiana State University. He thought constantly about the day he would be in college and on the university playing field. Right now he had two strong sports, baseball and football. So much would depend on how much he grew.

Nathan looked now at his mother, Kathleen. Well her *name* was Kathleen, but no one called her that. Everyone called her Kate, except his dad. His dad had called her Katie; at least he had called her Katie when things seemed to be going well between them. Nathan noticed things like that even though no one knew how much he paid attention to people and the things they did, especially his parents.

His mother was exceptionally pretty, he thought, looking at her now. He got his green eyes from her, but the dark hair was from his dad. Kate's shoulder length red hair and her petite build had been gifts from her Irish grandmother. It was hard for a kid to recognize beauty in a parent, but Nathan knew his mom was beautiful. However, if growing big enough to play college sports depended on her size, he was in trouble. Nathan was almost as tall as his mom now and he was just twelve years old.

But then, there was his dad to consider. His dad was just over six feet tall and had dark hair and eyes. He had heard people talk about his father's black Irish looks and say that he was a "heartbreaker." Nathan had wondered then if they meant he had broken Kate's heart or Nathan's own.

Nathan thought again about what his dad might have contributed to him as an athlete. Of course it was hard to tell about his dad's built—his weight had fluctuated so much. Nate Matthews was an athlete though. Nathan had seen him play basketball with some of the teenagers on the courts in the neighborhood and even as an older guy his dad had been awesome!

Nathan's eyes narrowed as he thought about his dad. He had seen him only a few times in the last five years, since he was seven years old. Nate Matthews was a drug dealer, drug user, and all that go with it. He was doing hard time in the Louisiana Department of Corrections and he had been for the last five years.

Nathan looked again at his mother and tried to focus on what she was saying. Sometimes when he thought about his dad, it was like he could not even hear the people around him. Nathan's teacher had once called his name when he was thinking about his dad. "Nathan," she had said, "you are not paying a bit of attention to what I am saying!" She had been right, of course. In the days when his dad had first gone to prison, he thought about him a lot. After that, he had learned not to. He focused his attention on his mother.

Kate was standing at the sink, arms crossed, still holding the dish towel that had dried the dishes after dinner. She was looking at Nathan, expecting him to say something. "Nathan," she said. "Did you hear me? Are you listening?"

Coming out of his reverie in response to his mother's tone, Nathan spoke, "I am sorry, Mom. What did you say?"

"I said," Kate spoke firmly. "I said, your father is being released . . . he is coming home."

CHAPTER 3

"Coming home? Coming home *here*?" Nathan erupted.

Kate Matthews nodded agreement to her son. "Yes . . . he is coming here." She turned quickly and began to run water into an empty sink. Kate acted as if everything were settled.

"Why is he coming here?" Nathan demanded. "Can't he go somewhere else? We are doing fine here, now, without him. I don't want him to come here!"

Kate looked around the comfortable condominium. Everything was in place. Two bedrooms, den with fireplace, furniture—she and Nathan *were* doing fine . . . now. That had not been the case just after Nate had been arrested and sentenced to prison. Help from her parents and her own hard work had made a comfortable place in the world for Nathan and herself; and now, *now* Nate was coming home!

"Your father has to give an address for where he will be living to the Department of Corrections as a part of being released. He has to come here, Nathan. We are his family and he has no where else to go!"

"He can go *anywhere* else, Mom. He is not going to stay . . . you know that don't you? He won't stay. It will be just like before. If he comes here," Nathan threatened, "I am leaving. I will go and live with Nana." Nathan loved his grandmother and he knew that if there was anyone who wanted his dad anywhere else on the planet other than with his mom it was Nana, Kate's mother.

Kate considered her mother. Nana was going to be furious at Kate's decision. She had been glad enough when Nate had been removed from the life of her daughter and grandson. Kate dreaded Nana knowing that Nate would be returning.

"You are not going anywhere," Kate said firmly. "That will be enough of that kind of talk. We are going to allow your dad to stay here until he can find a place of his own and that is the end of it," Kate said. "Besides you are too young to remember much about when you dad lived here anyway. You just think you remember—it is only things you have been told."

"I was seven years old, Mom—seven! I remember plenty!"

"Well, do you remember the good things, Nathan? Do you remember going to ball games, and the zoo? The Sundays in the park? Your dad even helped to coach your coach-pitch team. Do you remember that?" Kate offered a weak smile to support her words.

"I remember when he got arrested at the park and put in handcuffs right in front of my friends. I remember that! Do *you* remember it, Mom?"

"He sounds different now, Nathan. He says he is in recovery, working the Program of Alcoholics/Cocaine Users Anonymous.

He's clean. You know that he has been in treatment programs almost from the day he was arrested, for the last five years . . ." Kate looked at Nathan now, hoping he would show some sign of softening his attitude.

He did not. "Dad has been in jail for the last five years, Mom. *Jail!* Don't you get it? He hasn't changed. He is not going to change! You are just going to start trusting him again and he is going to do the same thing all over again. He will start disappearing and then he will leave or get arrested again and everything will be exactly like it was before!" Nathan was furious and he was beginning to get loud.

"That's enough, Nathan," his mom said. "We are going to let your dad stay here until he gets a place—just until he gets a place of his own. That's it! No more talking about it." She threw the dish towel on the counter and walked out of the kitchen.

Nathan walked outside. He was really angry, but he knew that arguing with his mother any longer would only cost him privileges. He walked slowly down the street to the playground of St. Anne's Catholic Church. It was the church that he and his mother attended, the church where he had his first Communion-right after his dad had been arrested for the last time. Now he played in the softball league there and went to mass on most Sundays. He felt he should go to mass; Father Sean helped to coach the team and going to mass seemed to be the least he could do.

The playground was almost empty. There were only a couple of mothers with toddlers playing on the wooden "ship" that had been built by the parents of the community. He walked to the other side of the playground and sat down in an empty swing.

As his sneakers dragged through the dusty ground beneath the swing, he began to think about his dad. Too young to remember? Too young to remember how things were when his dad was around? "I don't think so, Mom" Nathan spoke aloud.

"I remember a whole lot more than you think I do!"

CHAPTER 4

It had been a great day for a seven-year-old LSU fan! The Tigers had been losing to Alabama, their biggest rival. Alabama was ahead by just six points, when in the final seconds of the game, a short pass over the middle had resulted in a touchdown that tied the score. The kicking team took the field and the efforts of the freshman kicker had placed the perfect kick between the goal posts for an LSU win. Life could not have been better for Nathan Matthews!

Nathan had watched the whole game on television and he was still glowing with excitement when he got into bed. His mom had told him that his dad might be home from work tomorrow and that they might go to the park for a picnic. The fall weather was cool and Nathan was looking forward to the day.

Nathan did not understand exactly what his dad's work was, but it seemed that he was home a lot sometimes and then gone for a few days. He knew, too, that his mother must not like his dad's job, because when his dad was away working, his mother seemed angry. Mostly when she was angry, she got very quiet and made a lot of noise in the kitchen. Now that he thought about it, she had made a lot of noise in the kitchen tonight. He had just been too excited watching the game to notice until now.

Nathan fell asleep quickly, dreaming of when he would play sports in college. He awakened with a start when something crashed to the floor.

"I can't believe that you are coming home like this again, Nate! What is *wrong* with you? Where have you been?" Kate Matthews was furious. Nathan had never heard her voice that way, even when she was angry with him.

"Give me a break, Kate!" Nate Matthews was saying. His voice was fast and slurred and it sounded to Nathan like his dad had bumped into something in the living room. "Just give me a break! I really don't need to hear this from you, Kate. It is not like I haven't heard it before!"

Kate was unrelenting. "I am sick of this, Nate. You are drinking and you are loaded. You leave to go buy cigarettes, you *say*, and we don't see you for five days! Five days! What am I supposed to do? What am I supposed to tell Nathan? He is getting too old to believe you are on a business trip."

Kate laughed, almost hysterically. "I guess you *were* on a business trip, huh, Nate? Just not the kind of *business* you want to tell your son about? And, oh yeah, you seem to be using your entire product!"

"What are we supposed to think, Nate?" she asked, "What are Nathan and I supposed to do?" Nathan could tell that his mother was beginning to cry as she said this. He slipped out of his bed and eased to the doorway where he could see into the room where his parents were arguing. They were both standing in the middle of the room, his mother was crying and his father seemed to be having a difficult time keeping his balance.

Nate's voice was low, "Please, Kate, just calm down. We can talk. I have decided that I need to control my use. I can control it, I know I can—just help me Kate, please."

"Control it?" she asked with disbelief. "Control a cocaine addiction? You are an addict, Nate, an addict and an alcoholic. You *can't* control it!" Kate was torn between anger and sheer amazement that Nate would continue to talk about control.

"Quit!" Please for our sake, Nate, quit! Get some help and quit now."

"You cannot love Nathan and me and do this to us," she added. "You say all the time you are going to cut back or even quit. YOU NEVER DO! How can you keep on doing this to us? How can you do it to yourself? You are going to get caught; you are going to go to jail! What will happen to Nathan and me then, Nate? I have started back to school. How will I even feed Nathan if you are not here? If you are in jail?"

"I am not going to jail, Kate. I know what I am doing. I know who to trust. I am smarter than most of these guys; I am careful. I do not take chances." Nate sat down in the large chair in the living room. He looked tired and for a minute, Nathan thought he was going to go to sleep.

Kate moved to stand in front of him. "I am going to leave you, Nate. I am taking Nathan and we are leaving. You got that? I am done with your drugs and I am done with you!"

Kate could not leave him. She could not take Nathan and leave him. Nate sprang to his feet, and grabbed her arms, turning her toward him. "No, you are not," he started, "you are not leaving."

His voice was scary. Nathan had never heard Nate speak that way. His father certainly never spoke to him that way. His voice sounded like a movie on television, the kind of movie his mother did not let him watch, one with a lot of shooting and crime.

"Take you hands off me, Nate," Kate said evenly. She was staring directly into his father's eyes. That was when his father let her go. Kate was not expecting such a rapid release, and it threw her off balance, causing her to stumble backwards. She fell over a footstool that sat at the edge of the chair. She tumbled backward, hitting her head on the corner of the table. Blood started to cover her hair.

Nathan started into the room, his small fists clenched, ready to do as much damage as an angry seven—year-old could inflict upon a drunken, high adult man. But something stopped him—it was his father's expression. As soon as his mother had fallen, his father appeared to be instantly sober. Fear registered on Nate's face as he moved across the room to reach for his wife, to help her. "Katie, Katie . . ." he began softly.

His mother was standing on her own now and moving away from his dad. Nate reached toward her. "Don't touch me," she hissed as she disappeared into his parents' bedroom, holding her hand to the wound on her head.

Nathan wanted to go after her, but he wanted even more to know what his father was going to do now. He watched him. Nate Matthews sank into the large chair in the den, put his head in his hands, and for the first time ever, Nathan saw his father begin to cry.

CHAPTER 5

When Nathan awoke the morning after witnessing his parents' bitter argument, he thought maybe he had been dreaming. He could smell coffee and bacon frying, and he could hear the lowered tones of his parents talking.

Nathan got up, wandered up the hallway, and cautiously entered the kitchen. His dad was sitting at the kitchen table, drinking coffee and reading the sports sections of the Times Picayune while his mother stood at the stove making breakfast. She was wearing a baseball cap, one that would cover a cut like the one he thought he saw the night before. Her eyes were red, as if she had been crying.

Nathan quickly looked at his father, remembering that he had been witness to Nate's tears as well. His father looked normal, maybe his eyes were a bit red, but they were red often. His dad had allergies—at least that is what he said. Both parents greeted him and his mother set a breakfast plate down in front of him.

"What about those Tigers, Nathan?" Nate said. "That was an exciting win, huh?"

Nathan looked from one parent to the other. They were acting like nothing had happened. "I heard you guys fighting last night," Nathan said. "Mom got hurt." He looked from Katie to Nate.

Nate folded the newspaper and reached to put his large hand over Nathan's smaller one. "Son, . . ." he began.

"Eat your breakfast, Nathan," his mother interrupted. "It is getting cold."

Nate removed his hand, stood up from the table, and left the room without speaking. Somehow that action on the part of his father made Nathan very sad. He looked at his mother for help in understanding, but she was already turning away to begin to wash the breakfast dishes that were waiting in the sink.

After that night, things got better, at least they got better for a while. His dad was at home more, except when he was gone a couple of hours at night for three or four nights a week.

"Where does Dad go every night, Mom?" Nathan had asked his mother.

"He is going to Meetings, Meetings at the church."

"What for?" Nathan insisted. He knew that some parents met with Father Sean to plan activities for kids, or build playgrounds. He liked to think that his dad might be doing that. Nathan knew that his dad could do a lot of things. He had worked as a welder, a carpenter, a roofer. He had even played guitar in a band. Nathan was very proud of his father. He wanted to be just like him.

Kate did not want to try to explain Alcoholics Anonymous to a curious seven-year-old like Nathan. She simply replied, "The Meetings help him with his problems."

Nathan looked around the kitchen. It was quiet now. His dad had not returned. "Who helps you with your problems?" He asked, wanting to think that his parents were treated fairly.

"You ask too many questions, Nathan," his mother said. She returned to her own devices.

As so, life had gone on. His father was gone a few nights a week for a while, and his dad was working now as a welder and coming home every day. Nathan had not heard any more arguments and he thought everything seemed fine. At least, things seemed to be fine for a while.

CHAPTER 6

Nathan was having trouble going to sleep. For the past few months, his dad had been coming into his room for a few minutes just before he turned out the light. They would talk about things—which teams might play in the bowl games, what they planned to do during the upcoming Christmas holidays, school. But his dad had not come home yet. It was Saturday night and Nathan wanted to talk with him about all the college games that had been played that day, but his dad was not at home.

Nathan could tell that his mother was worried and maybe a little angry. He hoped that they did not have another argument like the one before. He lay in his bed and tried to stay awake to be certain that he heard his dad when he came in and that everything was OK, but he finally drifted off to sleep and woke up only when he heard the door to the kitchen slam.

"Oh my god, Nate, what happened?" Kate said. Nathan could tell something was very wrong and he jumped from his bed and ran into the kitchen.

His father was there and he was bleeding from a cut above his eye. The other eye was swollen shut and he had multiple bruises on his face. His shirt was torn and he was holding one arm to his rib cage. His hands were bruised and bloody. Nathan realized his dad was high and had been drinking heavily

Nathan had never really been certain when someone was using drugs, except for what he had seen in the movies. Even though his mother disapproved, he was sometimes able to watch the movies she hated, or there were television shows that were about people using drugs. But for some reason, in some way, Nathan knew—he was certain that, at that moment, his dad had been using.

"We've got to go to the emergency room. That cut needs stitches and you probably have some broken ribs," Kate said with authority. Kate was studying nursing. She wanted to be a nurse anesthetist, someone who administers anesthesia during surgery. Reaching that level of her profession would assure that she would be able to provide for Nathan and herself. She could tell now that Nate needed medical attention.

"We are *not* going to the hospital," Nate said quickly. "I will be OK. I can't go to the hospital, Kate. They will do blood work, file a report." Even high, Nate's thinking was clear enough to be aware that he could not be found with drugs in his system.

Nathan must have realized that his dad was high before his mom had, because it seemed that she did not fully understand that until Nate told her he was not going to get any medical help. Maybe she was just so concerned with how badly he was injured that she looked over his altered state, but she could see it now.

'You *are* loaded!" Kate said and angrily pounded her small fist on the kitchen counter. "How could you do this *again*? You were doing so well—what happened?"

"There were three guys," Nate began, "and I owed them . . ."

"I don't mean what happened to get you beaten up; I mean what happened to get you loaded?" She was irate.

"I don't know, Kate, I really don't . . ." Nate said then his eyes focused on Nathan standing in the doorway. "Go back to bed, Nathan," Nate said.

"But, Dad," Nathan countered, trying to ask if he was all right.

Nate looked away from Nathan's innocent, concerned face, but he spoke very sternly. "I said go to bed. Get out of here, now, Nathan!"

Nathan quickly disappeared into his room. He had never heard that tone of voice, but he knew better than to argue. Just before shutting the door to his bedroom, he looked back at his parents.

His mother was holding her mouth in the tight expression that even Nathan recognized as anger, but she was wiping the blood from his father's face.

CHAPTER 7

Nathan continued to sit for a long time in the playground swing and think about the way life had been when he was just seven years old, the way life had been before his dad had gone to prison. After his father had been beaten, he remembered, things seemed all right at home for a while. Nate had stayed in the house until the bruises on his face healed. Nathan was amazed at how long that had taken. At first, his father's face was swollen with deep purple bruises. Later the bruises were yellow and green, and the swelling went down slowly. After a day or two, Nate had gone to the hospital where the doctors there had confirmed Kate's suspicions that he had broken ribs—three, in fact. Nate told the doctors that he had been in a wreck. Nathan wondered, now, if the doctors had believed that story or if they just treated so many people whose stories seemed strange that it did not really matter.

His parents were not fighting then, at least if they were, Nathan could not tell. They were polite to each other. Really-they seemed almost too polite. When his dad's face had healed, he began to go out more. Nathan could tell that his ribs still caused him pain, because Nathan saw Nate wince when he moved suddenly.

It took very little time before Nate started staying away for a few days at a time again. His mother was quiet, the "angry" quiet that Nathan had come to recognize. But even with all the telltale signs, Nathan had been shocked when his father had been arrested. His mother had been very upset, crying for hours at a time.

Kate had tried to talk with her family about her feelings about Nate being arrested. When she had told her mother that she was angry, worried, and frightened for Nate, his grandmother had advised Kate to forget about his dad. "You and Nathan are better off without him," Nana had said.

After his father went to court, it was apparent that he would not be coming home for some time. Nathan could still remember his mother telling him that his dad would be gone for five years. It had been the last time Nathan had remembered crying.

Even so, Nathan did not fully understand. Nate had times before when he had gone to court, Nathan knew. Usually he was gone a few weeks and then back home again. "Can't he come home earlier, like he always did before?" Nathan had asked.

"Not this time, thank god," Nana had said. Kate had stilled her with a look. "Your father will be gone for five years . . . but we will be OK. We will be OK," Kate said again as if to reassure herself. Nathan realized, then, that he would be twelve years old when his father was able to come home.

Nathan's thinking about the past was interrupted when he saw his friend, Mindy, coming toward him. She was on roller blades, complete with helmet and knee pads. She needed them both, he thought, because she was flying down the sidewalk.

Mindy had been Nathan's best friend ever since they had started kindergarten when both were five years old. Neither Nathan nor Mindy had "whole" families now and that seemed to be a bond between them. Her mom had died when Mindy was born and she lived with her father, who was a New Orleans firefighter, and with her older brother Jake. Jake was sixteen and went to the new high school that had been built in their neighborhood. The old school was now a middle school and Nathan and Mindy both went there. Next year, they would join Jake as high school students themselves.

"'Why are you sitting here in this swing? It is almost dark . . .'" Mindy asked. Mindy's father and Nathan's mother were alike in one thing. When the street lights came on, you had better be at home, or at least in your own courtyard.

"He is coming home," Nathan answered, as if explaining that his father was coming home would explain why he was sitting in this little "kid" swing in the playground at dusk.

It did. Mindy did not have to ask who was coming home. She and Nathan had talked enough about his father for her to know instantly. Nathan had confided to Mindy during the Storm how really worried about his father he was. The news reports said that some of the men who were prisoners in New Orleans were locked in jails and left behind when the water began rising. Nathan just could not imagine that the father he remembered would not find a way to save his own life, and the lives of others if they were threatened. There were things about his dad he had really admired and being smart in an emergency was one of them.

But still, the news reports were bad, and Nathan had told Mindy how scared for his father he really was. Mindy was a very practical little girl and she recognized when it was time to get help from adults. She had gone to her own father and he was able to get more information than most people because of his connections as a firefighter. After a week or so, Mr. Thomas had reported that Nate Matthews had survived the Storm. He had gone through some rough times, but he was safe in Texas with the group that had been evacuated to the federal facility.

"When," Mindy asked. "When is he coming home?"

"I'm really not sure. I kind of had a fight with my mom when she told me. I was so mad, I didn't even ask her when," Nathan admitted.

"You better find out," Mindy said. They began their walk home then, Mindy moving slowly on the skates and Nathan jogging beside her.

CHAPTER 8

Kate Matthews looked out the window. It was almost dark and Nathan knew he had to be in by streetlights. Where was he? she wondered. He had been upset when he left, and she had hated that, but she had to let Nate come home. She did not know what else she could do.

Kate had tried to put Nate completely out of her mind during the time he had been away. So many people had hinted or advised that he was trouble, but something deep inside Kate kept telling her differently. She really could not understand her attraction to him, but she knew it had always been present, undeniably.

Through it all, the elementary and high school years, Kate had been drawn to him as to no other. She had no intention of letting him back into her life now. Kate was doing too well to risk a life with Nate again. She agreed with her mother that everything was so much less chaotic with him away, but she just could not deny him a place to stay until he was able to get settled on his own; and after all, Nathan was his son, too. He would need to see Nathan.

Even certain that she would not allow herself to be drawn to him again, Kate was nervous about his coming home. She understood Nathan's uneasiness.

She was still watching out the window when Nathan and Mindy came into view. Kate could not help but smile at the sight of them. Mindy was truly Nathan's best friend. She was a precious child, Kate thought, and beautiful, too. She had hair the color of honey that hung down her back when she did not have it confined in a pony tail that protruded from the back of her baseball cap. Even then, the curls escaped, reminding anyone who saw her that Mindy Thomas was a beauty-in-waiting. Mindy's eyes were large and blue and set at just the right proportion for her perfect face, and they were usually focused on Nathan.

Kate wondered when Nathan might realize that Mindy was a beauty—or even a girl. He had his mind on sports, not girls. Kate smiled again. It was a precious time of life when friendships could exist between the opposite sexes without complications of romance. Right now, Nathan just knew that Mindy was one girl who could catch a baseball or shoot hoops at the neighborhood court as well as some guys. Mindy and Nathan were inseparable. Where you found one, you found the other. She wondered if Nathan talked to Mindy about Nate. I hope he does, Kate thought. Nathan was going to need a friend.

Kate watched them now, saying good-by and planning where and when they would meet tomorrow. They reminded her of herself and Nate in the early years. She had loved Nate the first time she had laid eyes on him when he had come to her school in the middle of the school year as a fifth grader. Already taller than most and athletic, Nate attracted her even then and she could not really define why. They became friends, walking home from school together, talking about everything. She managed to go to most of the ball games Nate had played and she seemed to have a romantic interest in him long before Nate had come to think of her as a girl.

She had kept that interest to herself, concealing it from Nate and allowing their friendship to grow strong before they ever became a couple. That was long ago, but even then, Nate had secrets.

Kate remembered the times when Nate would come to school with a black eye, or when he would not change to gym shorts before playing ball in physical education classes. He had told her that his dad was a mean drunk and that sometimes Nate had to step between his father and mother to keep his mother safe. Kate told no one Nate's secrets—not then and not now.

There was one time when a teacher had noticed Nate's bruises and reported the family to social services. Nate had begged him not to do it; and when he had missed school the following day, Kate had almost lost her mind with worry. Nate confessed later that he had gotten one of the worst beatings of his life when he was finally returned to his parents' home. He had tried to tell his father that he had not asked for help, that he had denied the abuse; but by that time his father was already drunk. The protests—the truth—had not mattered.

"I will never hurt my kids, or my wife," Nate had told her while they were still children. And he never had. The only fight that Kate had seen Nate have had occurred when they were a young couple visiting friends. She had been pregnant with Nathan at the time and they had been invited to visit the couple to cook out on the Fourth of July.

During a simple conversation the wife had disagreed with her husband about a story he was telling and he had told her to shut up. The wife had been embarrassed, probably because they had guests, and had tried to correct him again. That was when her husband had slapped her, hard—across the face.

Nate had overturned the table in his lunge for the abusive husband. He hit him once in the lower jaw and then reached for Kate's hand. "We are leaving," Nate had said and they had stepped over the spilled tomatoes, pickles, onions, and chips on their way out.

They were never with that couple again. Nate could not abide violence, she remembered. She wondered, sadly, how he had tolerated violence in prison. Would everything about him be different now? she wondered.

Suddenly, Nate's son was standing before her. She had not heard Nathan come in. "So," Nathan asked, "When is he coming home?"

CHAPTER 9

"You could have told me yesterday that I had only one day to get ready for this," Nathan said to his mother. "How long have you known? I really did not have time to get ready."

Kate said nothing and chose only to look at him. Nathan looked back at her. She looked as if *she* had taken plenty of time to get ready, he thought grimly. Kate had on just a touch of make up and her hair was styled perfectly. Her green linen shirt just exactly matched her eyes and the fitted jeans emphasized her youthful figure. Most of the time, she did not take time for such careful dressing. She looked pretty without all the effort. Today she looked great.

The bus station was in a bad part of town. It was easy to spot from the interstate and Kate maneuvered the car into a parking space and she and Nathan went into the building.

"He left on the first bus out this morning," Kate said, looking around nervously. "Since north Louisiana is about six hours by bus, he should be getting here any minute."

Nathan said nothing. The two of them sat down and waited, watching the clock and watching the terminal. People were coming and going and Nathan wondered if he would have any difficulty recognizing his father. Then, suddenly, there he was. Nate Matthews stepped off the bus, dressed in jeans and a bright, white tee shirt. Nate was smiling. "He looks so healthy," Katie said, already moving toward him.

She was right, Nathan thought. His dad was in shape. Actually it was obvious that he had been in weight training, though he was not bulky looking, just solid. He carried no extra body fat. Nate's hair was cropped short in the latest style and he was tanned, as if he had been working outside, or even at the beach. He carried one small bag.

Nate saw them instantly and the smile that he carried became even warmer. He dropped the bag to give Kate the first hug. Nathan noticed that the top of his mother's head just exactly fitted under his father's chin. His parents held their embrace, and Nathan heard his dad say only one word. "Katie," he said as his eyes closed for a moment.

Then Nate was letting Kate go and reaching for Nathan. Nathan stepped up, allowing himself to be hugged. As his father's powerful arms went around him, Nathan felt a surge of unexpected emotion. Nathan felt safe, and until that moment he had never realized he needed to feel safer. He felt as if some of the burden of responsibility he had been bearing, without even realizing it, was lifting off him as he stood there in his father's embrace.

Tears sprang to Nathan's eyes. He thought for a moment that he was going to lose it completely and cry like a baby. He clung to Nate longer than he had intended, hoping to gain control. He felt his chest begin to heave; the sobs were coming . . .

Nate felt it too and hugged him tighter. In a moment, the emotion was gone from Nathan as suddenly as it came. Nate was letting go as Nathan pulled away. Still shaken, Nathan turned his attention to this father's bag. He lifted the light bag and headed toward the car.

"Do you want to drive?" Kate asked Nate. He smiled and moved toward the passenger side of the car.

"No license," Nate said, smiling.

Nathan climbed into the back seat.

"Let's go home," Nate said, the family headed up the ramp to the interstate.

CHAPTER 10

"I'm hungry," Nathan said, just as the car had settled comfortably into the center lane of traffic on the interstate. "We didn't eat breakfast."

"Yes, you did," Kate said. "You ate cereal." Then, to Nate, "He is always hungry!"

"I want some *real* food," Nathan argued. "Let's go to McDonald's."

Nate laughed, "*Real* food, huh? At McDonald's . . . Let's stop, Kate. I could eat too."

Kate began moving the car toward the right, ready to exit as the golden arches came into view. The three of them entered the restaurant just as a busload of senior citizens was getting settled at most of the tables. They had their food and coffee.

Nathan ordered pancakes, with sausage and eggs. He ordered hash browns and orange juice as well. Both Nate and Kate had a biscuit with sausage and coffee. As they settled down to eat, Nathan looked around the room. *I bet none of these people would believe* that we just picked my dad up from five years in prison, he thought. He looked at his parents, sitting there at the table with him. He could not help thinking that they looked like a regular family.

"Tell us what you did on the work release program," Kate urged Nate. She knew that he had been working for several months because he had been sending money home to her. It was a program that was designed to help the men who had been incarcerated make a better adjustment once they were released.

"I worked for a farmer, a farmer who owned and farmed a lot of land. Actually, I worked a lot in the farm office, doing computer work, but sometimes, I was able to help with some of the other chores. I enjoyed it," Nate replied.

"Did you have to go back to jail at night?" Nathan asked. When Kate gave him a stern look, he realized that his question might not have been the best thing to ask. He had not meant to be rude, but he wondered if his dad had been free to work outside the prison, why he had not just come home to work.

"It's OK," Nate said to Kate, and then, "Yes, Nathan, everyone on work release has to return to lock down at night. It is not real freedom, just a test of freedom. It helps offenders, especially those who are addicts like me, test their ability to stay with their sobriety program. Getting drugs or alcohol is much easier in work release, and of course, there is constant drug screening, but it is a good way to start recovery on the outside. In a way it makes serving time harder though. I missed you and your mother even more, but I was glad to be able to earn some money, some honest money."

When Nate had said "missed your mother" Kate had gotten up to go for more coffee. It seemed to make her terribly uncomfortable.

Well, Nathan thought, at least his dad was not going to back away from talking about his prison experience. That would make it easier, if everyone did not have to tip toe around, acting like nothing unusual had happened for the last five years. "I want some more orange juice," Nathan said getting up and returning to the line in front of the counter.

"He's grown up a lot," Nate said to Kate who was returning to the table as Nathan left it. "I can't wait to see him play ball. Does he eat like this all the time?"

"You bet," she said. "I can hardly keep him in clothes he is growing so fast." She instantly regretted saying it. It could seem to Nate that she was complaining about having to do it alone financially, at least until very recently when he had started work release. Nate smiled, apparently not offended.

"It's OK, Katie," he said. "Relax, it's just me!"

Nathan looked back at his parents as he stood in the line waiting to place his order. They were talking, smiling at each other. Nate looked like he was trying to memorize every detail of his wife's face. He did not take his eyes away for a minute.

Kate was attentive to his father too, but she was being careful. Nathan recognized that his mother was holding something back. She was a little nervous and kept pushing back a loose strand of hair that slipped to her face. She did that sometimes when she was ill at ease, Nathan knew. He knew just about every thing about his mother's moods. He wondered if his dad knew too.

Good luck, Dad, he thought and then wondered why he was thinking that. Nathan was not even sure he wanted his parents to reconcile. His mother had said, "your father will be staying with us for a while until he can find a place of his own." Now that did not sound as if she were planning for things to continue the way they had been before his dad left. Nathan knew that his parents were not divorced and he was glad. Father Sean had said that it is always better if the people in a marriage try very hard to work things out, that divorce was an option only if someone was being hurt or abused. He wondered if his parents were thinking of divorcing now.

If it could be like it is now, it would be all right, Nathan thought. If his dad would not drink or use drugs, or go out with those friends that his mother did not like. If only his mom would not be so angry and fuss at his dad so much. If they would do that, then maybe, they could be a real family. Nathan thought he knew what they both should do to make them a family, but no one asked him. No one was telling him anything about what their real plans were and that made Nathan a bit angry. He felt like he was the one who was going to be affected the most by their decisions, and no one was asking him anything. Kids were never treated fairly in things like this, he thought.

Nathan returned to the table just as his parents were finishing their coffee. "Ready?" he asked. "Let's go." He could not wait to get home and talk all this over with Mindy.

CHAPTER 11

As the car got closer to the old neighborhood that Nate recognized, he grew quieter. His attention was drawn to the activity on the street and he felt, for a moment, the old conflict of emotion that had enveloped him for so long, the old battle between right and wrong, between Good and Evil. He was grateful for the changes in himself and terrified that he could not sustain them. Nate took a deep breath and remembered that he did not have to do it alone, he had the strength of his Higher Power to guide him this time.

Nate thought about the term, *Higher Power*. It was a recovery term straight out of the Big Book of Alcoholics Anonymous. Every time Nate thought Higher Power, he thought Jesus crucified, Jesus suffering for the sins of mankind, Jesus suffering for the sins of Nate Matthews. The use of the term Higher Power was offensive to some who were Christians like Nate, but not to him. He recognized the need to describe the Spiritual Awakening essential to recovery in a way that would exclude no one.

Nate just had a different way of thinking about it after discussions with his counselor who also shared Nate's religious convictions. "I think use of the term Higher Power," she said, "has made it possible for so many to seek the 12-Step program who might have been offended if a certain belief were presented as the only one. I would imagine," she continued, "that countless people in need of recovery have entered the Program not knowing Christ and have continued in the program and come to know Him. God does work in mysterious ways to reconcile mankind to Himself."

That had settled it for Nate, not that he accepted her thinking, but that she had been able to articulate what he had come to believe on his own. He could think of more than a few men who had done just what she had described.

Even knowing his counselor's strong beliefs, Nate had seen her work, leading group after group, individual after individual. She always spoke in such a way to allow every man the right to his own creed, his own understanding of spiritual guidance. But each time a new treatment group was formed, eventually Nate had heard someone ask her, "What do *you* believe?"

Her answer was always the same, "It is important that I be honest with you and I would be dishonest if I claimed to believe anything other than the message of Jesus Christ. That is my Truth—you are free to have your own."

"Just provide the Holy Spirit with a forum and trust God to do the work," she had advised Nate later. "We don't have to do everything." He had found that her suggestions had worked for him as well.

These were Nate's thoughts as Kate was parking the car under the covered parking and the family was emerging. "This is a nice place near the old neighborhood, Kate," Nate said as she unlocked the door to the townhouse and they all went inside. "You have worked hard to provide for our family. I am sorry you had to do it alone. There has been so much pressure on you."

"It's OK," she said. "We are doing OK now." It sounded like she was trying to convince someone, Nathan thought. It definitely implied that there had been some time when they had not been 'doing OK.' Nathan remembered the time when he and his mother had lived with her parents, when she had first returned to school to become a licensed practical nurse. She had studied hard and was gone a lot and Nathan remembered the times with his Nana and Pop as fun times . . . maybe they had not been such fun times for his mother.

When his mother had gotten her first job at the hospital, she had kept on going to school. She did a lot of course work on line, staying at the computer late into the night and rising early to work again the next day. She had gone to some seminars that lasted all weekend and then returned to work on Monday without even a day off. After a couple of years, she had become a registered nurse. That was when they had been able to move out of his grandparents' house and get a place of their own.

Kate was in school again to become a nurse who could give anesthesia. His mother had told him that would really help them financially, when she was able to complete that certification. The trouble was, she had to keep working while she went to school and it made it take longer.

"We're OK," Nathan heard her say again to his father. "Nathan is in Catholic school and he has some good role models in Father Sean and his coaches. They spend a lot of time with him."

Nathan noticed that this made his father look away. It seemed that what she was saying was painful for him to hear. "Father Sean is still here then?" Nate said, even though he knew very well already. Nate remembered when Father Sean had paid him a visit when he was active in his addiction and tried to warn him that he was in trouble, that he needed to change his behaviors and return to the faith of his childhood. He was at risk of losing Kate and Nathan, the priest had said. "I've got some amends to make with Father Sean," Nate said.

"Amends, what do you mean 'make amends'?" Nathan asked. They were seated now in the den of the apartment. It was comfortably furnished. An entertainment center hid the television and stereo, making the fireplace the focal point of the room even in summer. Nate could imagine how Kate must have decorated for Christmas, hanging stockings on the mantle and placing the tree nearby.

"When you are an addict—and I *am* an addict *and* an alcoholic," Nate explained, "part of your recovery program is identifying the people you have hurt or wronged in some way and telling them you are sorry, *making amends,* if possible. It also includes making changes in your life so that you do not make the same mistakes again."

"You hurt Father Sean?" Nathan said, unable to believe that anyone could ever want to hurt a man like the gentle priest he had come to love.

"I lied to him, *often*," said Nate. "He tried to help me and I repaid it with lies."

"Oh," said Nathan. He needed more information about this recovery thing. "Can I ask you something else?" he said.

"Shoot," Nate replied.

"You said you *are* an addict and an alcoholic. I thought you *were* an addict. Mom said that you had quit using drugs and drinking." Nathan was confused and scared.

"I will always be an addict and an alcoholic." Nate explained patiently. "That doesn't mean I am using or drinking. It means that I have no power over drugs or alcohol. I cannot control it. I have to live my life not drinking or using drugs at all."

"So you will never drink or use again . . ." Nathan asked.

"I have recognized that I cannot manage my addiction, so each day I ask for the help of my Higher Power, God, to keep me from using or drinking that day," Nate explained.

"Oh, brother," Nathan interrupted. This was going to be worse than he thought. Why couldn't his dad just promise him that his life as an addict was over?

"I know it is confusing, son," Nate explained. "I will be telling you more about it—how it works. I think that when you understand the program better, you will know how it can work for me and for our family. You see, addiction is a family illness. It affects all of us. You and your mother have certainly been affected by it for the last five years. We all need to learn about it, we need to learn what we can do to make our family work." Nate glanced up at Kate. She pretended not to listen.

Nathan was really listening. He wanted to understand this stuff and it sounded very interesting. Just as he and his dad were really focusing on the discussion, his mother interrupted. "I made crawfish fettuccine, Nate," she said. "I did not think you would want to go out."

Nate recognized an old pattern and he knew he would need to get his family into recovery programs of their own very soon; but this was not the time to belabor a point. His counselor had warned him about taking things slowly. "Remember that *you* are the expert on recovery. Your family does not know what you know. Honesty and patience are the most important things when you first go home," she had said.

Nate had been honest with Nathan. Nate knew it would take much more explanation before his son, and his wife, began to understand the program of recovery that AA and CA provided. Honesty and patience, he thought. Right now it was important to eat some of Kate's crawfish fettuccine and like it!

It was a wonderful meal. Nate had thought about the good Cajun cuisine that south Louisiana offered when he was locked away in north Louisiana, eating institutional food. Kate was a good cook and she had done her best. Nathan ate, again, as if he were starving.

He looked at his son. "Where does he put it all?" he asked Kate in disbelief when Nathan filled his plate again.

"He's very active—always practicing something," she said.

When the meal was finished and Nate and Nathan had done the dishes, Nate asked, "Is there a video store nearby?"

"Just down the street . . . why?" Nathan asked.

"There's a movie I'd like you guys to see," Nate said, "if we can find it. Have you seen *Clean and Sober?*"

Kate and Nathan shook their heads.

"Well, I have to go to a Meeting. There is one in the church building just down the street in twenty minutes. I'll be back in about an hour and a half . . . why don't you guys go get the movie and we'll watch it when I return?" Nate said.

"You are going out?" Kate asked. Nathan watched her. She looked alarmed, scared, and a little angry. Nathan was trying to make sense of the emotions floating around in the room between his two parents and he could not.

"Katie," Nate said softly, "I am going to a Meeting, no where else. I promise."

Nathan noticed that his mom was clenching her hands. What was happening? He looked at his father.

"I have to find a sponsor. I have to do this, Katie. I am an addict, an addict in recovery. Just try to trust me—just a little," Nate said.

Even as confused as he was, Nathan realized that his father was not asking his mother's permission. He was just gently telling her that he was going out and would be back—back in an hour and a half. He watched his mother. She nodded her head in agreement and Nathan could tell she was fighting tears. She had nodded because she could not speak. His father had been home less than six hours and already he had made her cry!

CHAPTER 12

Kate was uneasy. She tried to busy herself reading a magazine, then folding laundry, but she was watching the clock. When she finally moved to the computer, Nathan could see that his mother was still upset and wondered why she did not believe his dad when he said he would return within an hour an a half. Nathan was relieved when his father came walking through the door about ten minutes earlier than he had promised.

Kate saw him come in as well. She observed him carefully and Nate knew she was assessing to see if he had been drinking or using drugs. Confident that he was straight, she smiled warmly, "Hi, Nate, we got the movie," she said. "I'll make nachos for us to eat while we watch it."

Nathan put the DVD into the player and reached for the remote. He stretched out on the floor and his dad sat on the sofa. When Kate came into the room, she settled into a large chair. "What's this movie about, Dad?" Nathan asked.

"Addiction, about an addict and his disease of addiction. I think you will find it interesting," Nate replied.

As the family followed the action of the movie and watched as the main character struggled to get past the denial of thinking he did not have a problem with drugs or alcohol and moved into recovery from his addictions, Katie and Nathan were spell bound. The final scene, with the lead character in an AA meeting, proudly displaying his AA chip that represented thirty days of sobriety, was deeply moving.

"Did Michael Keaton win an Academy Award for that role?" Kate asked Nate. "He was wonderful. He had the mannerisms of an addict down perfectly."

"He is good," Nate responded.

"Do you have a chip, Dad?" Nathan asked. Nate dug into his pocket and produced the chip he had been given only an hour earlier. He handed it to Nathan.

"It's a twenty-four-hour chip," Nate explained. "I have five years of abstinence and about three and half years of real sobriety in prison, but once you leave prison, you start over."

"Why?" Nathan asked.

"Because it is easier to stay abstinent in prison than on the street," Nate said.

"I thought that everyone in prison was drug free," Nathan said.

Nate smiled, "Nope. It is not hard to get drugs or alcohol in prison."

"What do you mean five years of abstinence and three and a half years of sobriety?" This time it was Kate who was asking. Nate was pleased that his family was already so interested in learning about the disease and recovery.

"Just because someone is not using drugs or alcohol does not mean they are working the program or in recovery. The AA/CA 12-Step Recovery Program teaches people who suffer from addiction how to live sober. It is really more about living sober than about how to not use," Nate explained.

"Is that what is meant by a *dry drunk*?" Katie asked, remembering some things she had learned in her training as a nurse.

"Exactly," Nate replied. "If an addict/alcoholic is just not using or drinking, but is continuing in the same behaviors, acting the same," he said to Nathan, "then he is experiencing a dry drunk. That is why the meetings and a sponsor are so important."

"What's a sponsor?" Nathan asked.

"Your sponsor is someone that you choose to help you work the 12-Step program. He—an addict chooses someone with the same sexual preference as his own—is there to tell you what you are doing right and what you are doing wrong. He is someone who is a recovering addict himself and has several years of sobriety. An addict can call on his sponsor at any time," Nate said.

"Do you have a sponsor yet?" Nathan asked.

"Not yet," Nate said. "I'll be getting one soon."

"It is getting late," Kate said. "I have to work tomorrow." She disappeared into the hallway to get blankets and a pillow from the linen closet in the hall. Coming back into the living room, she dropped the bed clothes onto the sofa.

"Nate," she said, "You can get Nathan to sleep on the sofa if you would rather sleep in his bed . . ."

Nathan looked from parent to parent. Things were suddenly very tense. "No that's OK, I will sleep on the sofa," Nate said. "Nathan needs to sleep in his own bed."

"Good night, then," Kate said. She turned quickly and disappeared into the master bedroom. She shut the door. Nathan and Nate stood looking at the closed door. Nathan turned to look at his father's face. Nate's face was smiling, but his eyes looked tired and sad when he answered to the door, "Good night, Kate."

CHAPTER 13

"How can you make almost all A's in school and be so dumb?" Mindy asked Nathan. Her blue eyes were flashing and she appeared to be very frustrated. "Your mom hurt your dad's feelings—that's what was going on. She hurt his feelings when she made him sleep on the sofa."

Nathan had explained to Mindy that everything had seemed to be going well between his parents until bedtime. Then there was so much tension. "She told him he could sleep in my room and I would sleep on the sofa," Nathan said, still not getting the whole picture.

"Gee whiz, Nathan. Married people sleep in the same room. Your parents *are* still married, aren't they?"

"Yes, they are married," Nathan replied, a bit indignant. He was beginning to understand. "You mean my dad thought . . ."

"Of course he did, exactly . . ." Mindy said. "Your mom might as well have thrown him out the front door. What did he say?"

"Nothing, he said nothing," Nathan answered. Then thinking about it further, he added, "He did look sad though."

"So, how were things this morning?" Mindy asked.

"OK, I guess. Mom went to work as usual. She did cook a big breakfast and Dad said he was going to look for a job, go to a Meeting, and try to find a sponsor."

"What's a sponsor?" Mindy continued to question.

"Later, I will tell you later," Nathan said as Jake, Mindy's older brother joined them.

Jake was sixteen and very cool. He was slim and was going to be tall, like Mindy's father. He had been a skateboarder, but lately had given up his skateboard and sometimes rode around in a car with an older friend. Mindy had told Nathan that her father did not like the older guys that Jake was hanging out with, but Jake did it anyway. He just hoped that his father would not find out.

"S'up?" Jake asked. He knocked Mindy's baseball cap off her head as he walked by. Nathan did not think much of that action, but Jake was too much older for him to do much about it—besides, he was her brother. Jake did pick up the cap and put it back on her head.

"Nathan's dad is at home," Mindy said.

"Really?" Jake said. "So is your pitching going to improve now?" he asked Nathan.

"What?" Nathan said, not knowing at all what Jake meant.

"Are you going to start getting advice on you pitching from the your dad, the star athlete?"

Nathan said again, "I don't know what you are talking about . . ."

Jake could see that Nathan really did not know what he meant. "Don't you know your dad was an all state pitcher in high school? He was offered a full scholarship to play at LSU and probably a bunch of other colleges."

"You are kidding," Nathan said. "Really? I had no idea . . . how do *you* know this?"

"His picture in his uniform with all his high school stats engraved on the award is in the trophy case at the high school. There is a picture of him with Skip Bertman when he was signing for a scholarship," Jake said.

Nathan had seen the trophy case at the high school, but it was full of trophies and awards. He had never really looked at all the plaques inside. He certainly had never seen his father. He was shocked. "Are you serious?" he asked again for certainty.

"Go see it yourself," Jake said. "His name, Nate Matthews, it's on the trophy."

Mindy could see how this was affecting Nathan. He was embarrassed at not knowing, and he felt betrayed. "Are you going to ask him about it?" she asked Nathan as soon as Jake left.

"No-no way! I'm just going to see how long he'll hide it from me," Nathan said. "He says he is honest. Let's just see how honest he really is."

CHAPTER 14

The sun was getting lower in the sky when Nate walked through the playground on his way to the ball field in the park. He was tired. Today had been his first day of work and although he was very pleased to have found such a good job so quickly, his aching muscles told him that the type of work he had done today was not what he was accustomed to doing. Fortunately his welding skills seemed to have gotten better—or maybe he was a better welder sober. Whatever the reason, today had been a good day at work.

He smiled to himself, thinking about the questions the boss had asked him at the interview. "Are you going to stay sober this time?" He had asked, because Nate had worked with him before he went to prison. He knew the kind of good work Nate was capable of doing, and he knew how Nate could mess up.

"I am going to stay sober today," Nate answered honestly. "I hope I will be sober tomorrow. I take it one day at a time now." Only when Nate was leaving work and he and his boss were walking into the parking lot did he notice the bumper sticker on his boss' truck. It read, "Another Friend of Bill's." Nate knew that meant a friend of Bill W.'s, one of the founders of the AA 12-step recovery program. Nate's boss laughed when he saw Nate reading the slogan. "See you at a Meeting," he had said.

His boss was recovering too. No wonder he had understood when Nate had told him he would stay sober one day at a time!

When Nate reached the field where Nathan's team was having their first practice for all stars competition, he stopped to lean on the fence along the third base line. The coach was pitching to team members who each took some time at bat; the others were in their fielding positions. Nathan was in the bull pen with two other pitchers and the pitching coaches were there instructing them with each pitch. Nate stayed where he was. He did not want to interfere.

Nate knew the coach who was pitching to the team members. His name was Justin; he was a year or two younger than Nate, but he had played on Nate's high school team *many* years ago, Nate thought with sadness. Justin was an attorney now, but Nate knew his love was still baseball. He had a son on Nathan's team.

When the teams took a water break, Justin joined Nate at the fence. Justin extended his hand. "Nate," he said simply.

"Justin," Nate replied.

"Quite a boy you've got, Nate," Justin said. They stood in silence for a few moments. "When did you get home?" Being an attorney who worked out of the DA's office, Justin knew where Nate had been, why he had been there, and for how long.

"A few nights ago," Nate said.

"You and Kate back together?" Justin asked. Nate knew that Justin had liked Kate when they were in high school. Justin had been born with every advantage that Nate had not. Despite the fact that Justin drove to school every day in a convertible BMW that had been a gift from his attorney dad on Justin's sixteenth birthday, Kate had chosen to walk home each day with Nate. Nate didn't understand it then and he really did not understand it now, but he was grateful.

"I'm staying there with Kate and the boy until I can find a place of my own," Nate replied.

"Sorry," Justin said and Nate hoped he meant it. "So, are you going to help us coach pitchers now that you are home?" Justin asked Nate as the boys returned to their positions in the field and the pitchers headed for the bull pen again.

"I am an ex-con," Nate said simply.

"Yeah," Justin said, "an ex-con and the best damned pitcher Northside High School ever fielded. If you had left the drugs alone, you'd probably be wearing a Yankee uniform with your picture on a cereal box."

"Never a Yankee uniform," Nate smiled. "The O's maybe, but never the Yankees."

"Will you help? We really need your help. We've got some talented kids, but our coaching is weak," Justin said.

"I'll have to talk to the boy about it," Nate said. "He doesn't know anything about my playing in high school."

"You're kidding. He really doesn't know you were offered full scholarships to LSU and ULM in Monroe? The pros were just waiting for you to finish college. He really doesn't know?" Justin asked. He was amazed.

"He was only seven when I left, and before that I was in and out of lockup on small charges. Talking to him about my failures wasn't high on my priority list," Nate said.

"Will you think about helping?" Justin asked again.

"I'll think about it," Nate said. "I will talk to Nathan. I don't want to embarrass him if he doesn't want me around."

"Good enough," Justin said. He shook Nate's hand again before returning to the field.

CHAPTER 15

Nate sat in the absolute quiet of the day just before dawn. He had risen from his bed on the sofa and moved outside to sit in the small enclosed courtyard that ran the entire length of the condo and opened onto the den and master bedroom. Kate had done a good job when she had purchased this home. It had all the amenities of a house, even the patio, partially covered by a large green awning. Everything was small, scaled-down, but ample for a mother and child who lived alone. It was clear to him now, the condo had not been purchased with his return in mind.

"I really don't fit here," Nate said to himself as he looked around the enclosure. It was filled with flowering plants and he sat now underneath the awning in one of the four chairs that matched the table. His six feet plus frame felt too big for the tiny space and Nate felt uncomfortable. He was beginning to feel sorry for himself.

During the few days that he had been at home, things had really gone pretty well, he thought. He had gotten a good job doing something that he liked and he was being paid very well.

Nathan seemed to be interested in learning more and more about his recovery experiences. And Kate, well, Kate was tolerating him. She was polite and kind and seemed to consider his feelings, but her behavior toward him defined distance. Generally she was treating him like the houseguest he was and it was getting in his hula hoop.

Nate thought about his hula hoop. During his treatment, his counselor had hung a child's hula hoop over the chalkboard. Each day she wrote an idea that supported recovery thinking inside the hula hoop. She explained that the addict needed to think of his sobriety as being inside his hula hoop. He, the addict, could let nothing, NOTHING, inside. Not death, or divorce, or rejection, or celebration, or *anything* could be allowed to penetrate the boundaries. The addict was safe in his boundaries if he understood that.

Clearly the hula hoop was a visual presentation of boundary enforcement. It worked for most of the men in treatment with him. It was not uncommon to hear someone move away from a confrontation on the prison yard by saying, "Man, you are getting in my hula hoop. Back off!"

Nate thought of some of the recovery phrases that had been inside the hula hoop and about their message for recovery.

"Once you have become a pickle, you cannot go back to being a cucumber," was a good way to remember that once a person has passed over into addictive drinking or use, there is no turning back. It would be impossible to try to practice "recreational" use ever again.

"It's not the caboose of the train that kills you," had much to say about the danger of the first drink or first drug to the recovering addict/alcoholic.

"If nothing changes, nothing changes," was a constant reminder of the necessity of commitment to a changed life.

"Time takes time," was the phrase on Nate's mind now.

"Time takes time," Nate said. How much time was Kate going to need? Again his counselor had tried to prepare him. "Just because you are in recovery, everything may not have the happy ending you hope for," she had said. "Your wife may *never* be willing to try again. You may have to move on."

His counselor continued in the spiritual context that she knew was meaningful for Nate. "The sin of your addiction has a cost and sometimes that cost is great. God forgives the sins of those who ask, but that does not mean we do not still have to suffer the consequences of our sin."

Nate was hurting. Throughout it all, even when she had accused him of not caring for her or Nathan, Nate had known that the love of his life was Kate. He closed his eyes in shame at some of the ways he knew he had betrayed that love in the height of his addiction. Kate had no idea that he had ever been unfaithful and his counselor had advised him not to tell her.

When his counselor had been certain that Nate was truly remorseful and understood that the integrity that comes with recovery would not allow infidelity in a relationship, she had cautioned him, "Why would you want to tell her something that would only make *her* feel worse and *you* feel better? Live with the pain of it yourself. Learn from it and do not burden her with more to suffer. It is going to be difficult enough without adding more for her to suffer."

His counselor had warned him on the day he had left, "I pray that you and Kate are able to restore your relationship." By this time, his counselor knew the major players in his life by name. "But if you can't, Nate, go on. Your son will always be your son, but Kate may not always be your wife. Watch your hula hoop on this one."

Nate just could not accept it yet. This was his Katie that they had been talking about. Nate knew Katie better than anyone and he knew that Katie loved him. He was tempted even now to walk into the bedroom where she slept, take her in his arms, and trust the old magic to win her back. It had always worked before and Nate knew it would work again.

Yet, he stayed in his chair on the patio. It could not be that way this time. If Kate returned to him, it had to be born of her own choice, not born of his coercion.

Kate needed her own recovery. She needed to understand that their relationship would be better when each stood alone in his own strength and then came together out of a healthy choice, not a needy one.

"I'm getting tired, God," Nate prayed honestly, "and I am lonely. I want my wife back. I am trying as hard as I can to do what you've asked me to do. I want her to treat me like she loves me again. I need help. Please, God, do something with Katie."

Immediately, Nate was reminded of the creation of woman from the rib of man. The scripture said that God had created a "helper" for man. He realized that is exactly what he needed in his relationship with Katie. He needed a helper, a partner, a friend, a companion, a lover.

As the first rays of sunlight began to light the sky, Nate prayed again, "Please, please don't let my addiction cost me Katie."

CHAPTER 16

"Who is this beautiful little girl that is Nathan's shadow?" Nate asked Kate. It was ten o'clock on a Saturday morning and they were having a second cup of coffee. Nate had been up for some time and had already folded the covers from his bed on the sofa. Kate had slept late and when she emerged from her bedroom she was glad to see that Nate had made French toast and sent Nathan on his way to ball practice. There were some things that were good about having two parents in the house, she thought. She had not slept this late for a very long time.

"That's Mindy," Kate said. "Was she here when Nathan left?"

"Yep," Nate said. "Was she going to practice with him?" he asked.

"Yeah, she'll just watch—from a distance. Kind of like . . ." Her voice trailed off.

"Kind of like *what*, Katie?" Nate asked, knowing what she had almost said.

"Nothing," she said and she started to get up from the table.

Nate caught her forearm. "Kind of like *what*?" he repeated. His deep brown eyes were focused on her face with an intensity. Kate turned away.

"Kind of like us, Nate, . . . kind of like we are, . . . were . . . , used to be . . ." She was confused and could not continue.

Nate let go of her arm. A smile came to his face and disappeared just as quickly. He decided to let her off the hook. "So does Nathan mind her being around all the time?"

"Doesn't seem to. Her mother is dead—died in childbirth when Mindy was born. She lives with her father, a fireman, and her older brother, Jake. I don't know about Jake, Nate. He worries me a bit. I see him a lot at school and neighborhood functions and he just always seems to be with the wrong crowd. I don't think he has a very good relationship with his father," Kate replied.

"Speaking of relationships with fathers, Justin asked me to help coach Nathan's team, coach the pitchers. What do you think?" Nate asked.

"That's great," Kate said with excitement. "I think Nathan will be pleased," Nate and baseball were two ideas that worked well in her thinking.

"Have you told him anything about me and baseball?" Nate asked her.

"No," Kate said. "I mean—why should I? You were away and what good would it have done for him to know? It would have only made him sad," she said.

"You didn't tell him because you didn't know what to tell him about how and why it all ended," Nate said. "That's why, isn't it, Kate? You don't know how to talk about my being an addict, about us being a family that has issues with addiction."

"*We* don't have issues with addictions, Nate. *You* do. There is nothing wrong with Nathan and me," she said.

"You are so wrong, Kate," Nate said. He had been dreading this discussion, yet knew they had to have it. "Addiction is a family illness, Kate, it affects all of us. I am in recovery; you need to get into recovery as well."

"Recovery from *what*? I am *not* sick," she said adamantly. "I can grasp that *you* have an illness. I remember how your father was with his drinking, I am not sick and Nathan is certainly not sick."

"Your father had some drinking issues, too, Kate. I learned in treatment that with the drinking issues your dad had, you were very likely to marry an addict or alcoholic," Nate began.

"Don't be ridiculous, Nate," she said.

"Just please go to Al-Anon when I go a Meeting. It is the group for people who are closely associated with addicts or alcoholics, people who are affected by someone else's addiction. You will learn there what I am talking about. Talk to the other men and women, those in relationships with addicts. They can explain it. Please, just try," he begged.

"I don't know, Nate . . ." she was set to refuse.

"What about your training as a nurse? What do they tell you in school about addiction?" Nate was trying very hard to find someway his wife could relate. He knew she had to admit to some knowledge from her nursing career.

"They *do* say it is a family disease, Nate, but I just don't see how that is me, or Nathan," she said.

"You don't see it is you because of denial, the same type of denial that I had to give up before I could get better. Please Kate, for all of us, think about going to a meeting with me," he looked at her with such intensity that she heard herself agreeing and was surprised by what she heard.

"OK, Nate, I'll go to a Meeting, one Meeting. If I don't like it, I won't go to another," she said.

At least that is a start, Nate thought. He was going to have to speak to his Higher Power about that meeting. "Please, God," he whispered, as Katie left the room. "When she goes, let that be a Meeting with people she can learn to trust."

CHAPTER 17

"I am terrified of him," Kate told Father Sean as she sat in his office at the church. "You know how hard I've worked to take care of everything while he was away. Now that he is here, I am so afraid of losing everything I've gained."

"What scares you, Kate?" the priest asked.

"I am afraid of asking him for help; afraid of depending on him for anything. Just last night, I was making a salad of tuna fish. Nate was sitting at the counter in the kitchen, talking with me and watching. I could not get the top off the jar of pickles. I tried, but it was too hard to turn. I ran warm water on it, I hit it with the handle of a knife, I tried to turn it with the rubber disk that is made to loosen jars. I just couldn't ask for his help."

"What did Nate do?" Father Sean asked.

"Nothing. He just watched me, didn't say anything. Finally, when I turned to put the pickles back into the refrigerator, he said, 'You don't want to put the pickles in the tuna fish, Kate?' I handed the jar to him then because I had to," she said.

74

"What happened?"

"He opened the jar with one twist and I put the pickles in the salad!" she said.

"That's good," the priest said. "No use letting pride spoil a good tuna fish sandwich!"

"I know, Father, I know how stupid that sounds, but *I'm* in control now. I just can't ask Nate for help," Kate said miserably.

"Why not?"

"Because, because . . . because what if I start to trust him again and he leaves again, or goes back out there with the drugs? I can't do it all again, Father. I just don't have it in me to do it again. I would rather be alone." she said.

"Would you?" the priest asked, thinking how little he had to say in this counseling session.

"Yes, yes, I would," Kate replied.

"You would rather be alone than risk taking a chance with Nate?" Father Sean said.

"Yes!" Kate looked determined.

"OK," Father Sean replied.

"OK, what?" Kate asked.

"OK, then be alone. I understand. You would rather be alone than risk being hurt by Nate again, right?"

"I know you trust him, Father. You think he has changed. I know you think that," Kate said.

"It doesn't really matter how *I* feel about Nate, Kate. What matters is how *you* feel about him. I can understand that you cannot risk it. I know how hard you have worked to provide for Nathan and support him without help from your parents. I would never ask you to give Nate a chance if you did not feel that you should," Father Sean said.

"Good," Kate said. "I am glad that's settled then." She seemed relieved. She looked around for her keys.

"Of course, there is just one problem . . ." the priest said, seeming to be more thoughtful than ususal.

"What's that?" Kate asked.

"You love him," Father Sean said, looking squarely in her eyes.

Kate looked stunned. She really had felt that her love for Nate was locked so far away that no one could see it or access it. "What do you mean?" she asked.

"I mean you love him," Father Sean said. "I really do understand if you decide that you cannot risk a life with him again. I remember how hard it was for you. Sometimes, especially at Christmas, you looked so pitiful there in the congregation with little Nathan beside you. It made me want to weep. I understand you cannot go there again. I am just saying to be honest with yourself. You can convince me you don't want a life with Nate, but will never convince me you don't love him."

"I was there from the very beginning, Kate. I remember how you were together as teenagers, how you nearly lost your way when you broke up for a while. I was there at the wedding, Nathan's birth, all of it," he said. "I have even watched you turn away the attention of other men while Nate was in prison. Some of them would have been good providers, good role models for Nathan. You were never interested. I guess I was wrong when I thought you were waiting to see if you could make things work with Nate."

Father Sean looked at her. Kate's eyes began to tear. Then, the tears spilled over.

"He's dangerous to me, Father," she whispered. "Sometimes I think Nate is more dangerous to me than the drugs are to him. If I let him back in, just a little, I am afraid I will lose me." Kate was able to get these words out with great difficulty between sobs.

"He probably *is* more dangerous to you than drugs are to him," the priest said. Kate, you need to go to Al-Anon. You need to understand where you stop and Nate starts. Al-Anon has some of the answers to the questions your heart is asking. Will you go?"

"I have already promised Nate I would go to one meeting," she said.

"It is unlikely than one meeting will be enough. Just give the meetings a try, Kate," Father Sean said.

"For Nate, . . . so that Nate can get what he wants, so that Nate can be happy?" she asked.

"No, . . . for Kate, for Katie," the priest said.

CHAPTER 18

"Coach wants you to help with pitchers," Nathan said. He had gotten up from the dinner table where he was having a late meal with his parents. He had walked behind the counter to pour more iced tea into his glass. His back was to his father when he asked, "You know anything about throwing a baseball?"

"A little bit," Nate answered.

Nathan returned to the table, sat his glass down firmly on the table and looked at his father straight on. He was angry, angry that this information about his dad's baseball career had been kept from him. It embarrassed him not to know. It seemed that everyone else knew. Why not him, he thought. His green eyes were full of anger and did not blink at all as he stared up at Nate's face.

They were locked there for a moment, the accused and the accuser, until Kate broke the silence. "Look, you two," she said. "Nathan, you obviously know now that your father played ball. He was all-state his junior and senior years. Nate, you know he knows—now, let's get on with it. Nate, are you going to help?"

"That depends on Nathan, whether Nathan wants me to help," Nate said.

"I don't really know how good you were, if you could really help the team," Nathan started.

Nate was getting angry. Nathan was playing some kind of game with him and not even telling him the rules. He felt like he was being interviewed by his twelve year old son for a job he was overqualified to do. Nate was trying to be understanding and honest, but he could not determine Nathan's hidden agenda. He needed to know and he could not figure it out. He felt his frustration growing, "I'm sorry I don't have a resume', son. It blew away during Katrina."

Kate recognized Nate's sarcasm as a bad sign and cautioned him with, "Nate."

'No, Kate, I am not going to sit here quietly and take this disrespect. Either Nathan wants me to help or he doesn't. Right now, I am pretty inclined to let him do it on his own." He was talking to Kate, but his eyes never left Nathan.

Nate's counselor had warned him about just such an incident as the one he was experiencing. Your son will have some anger toward you and he will be unlikely to tell you straight out. He will act out in some sort of way, sort of a test, to see if you, and your recovery, are real this time. Don't let him push your buttons," she had said. Nate felt as if Nathan were pushing all his buttons.

Katie walked out of the kitchen and left the two males still locked in their power struggle. "Nathan," Nate said, taking a deep breath. "I want to be honest with you. I would like to help, I would like for you to want me to help, to think that I have something valuable to share with you and the team. But I am not going to get involved if it is going to make things difficult between you and me. Our relationship is too important to me."

"I just don't really know what you can do," Nathan said. "It seems I've been kept in the dark about that. I would hate to bring in someone who really didn't know his stuff."

So there it was, Nate thought. Nathan felt that he had been treated unfairly. Anger was always about a perceived injustice. He looked at Nathan. Nathan was softening, but still angry that he did not know about his dad's high school career earlier.

Kate reentered the room holding a large cardboard box. "Here," she said, setting the box on the kitchen table. "Read this, Nathan, and decide if you think your dad can help."

Nathan looked at the box. It was covered with dust. He opened it carefully and saw that it was filled with newspaper clippings from fifteen years earlier. His eyes fell on the headline on the sports page. HIGH SCHOOL JUNIOR PITCHES NO HITTER TAKING NORTHSIDE TO PLAY-OFFS.

He lifted the article to find another. LSU OR ULM? MATTHEWS MUST CHOOSE. The box was full. He looked up at his father only to find that his father was looking at his mother.

"You've kept those all this time, Katie? he asked. Nate picked up a dried corsage out of the box. It had once been a baby yellow rose.

"Sports banquet?" he asked Kate. She nodded, remembering.

"Can I take this to my room?" Nathan asked. Both his parents turned their heads to look at him.

"Just don't lose anything," Kate said.

Nathan gathered up the box and started out of the door. "You can help, Dad," he said when he got to the door. "I want to win the citywide championship." He disappeared into the hall.

"Not, I want you to be involved, Dad," Nate said to Kate. "Just, I want to win."

"It's a start, Nate," she said. "I just wonder if you've still got the stuff."

CHAPTER 19

Nathan had not meant to eavesdrop on his parents 'conversation, it had just happened. He had carried the box containing the newspaper articles about his father's high school baseball career into his own room and shut the door. It took two hours, but he had read each article carefully, some he had read more than once. He had found a few notes his dad had written to his mom when they were teenagers, some cards, spirit ribbons, and a few pictures. His dad's pictures looked just like Nathan now, except Nathan had green eyes, rather that the brown eyes his father had. Both had dark hair.

Reading the articles made Nathan see his father in a whole new light. He had never thought much about what his father had been doing before he began drinking and using drugs. Now he was beginning to see that things had not always been the way that he thought.

Nathan closed the box and turned off his light. He wanted to return the box to the kitchen without running into either parent.

He was still embarrassed about the whole thing and he needed more time before anyone asked him any questions about what he had read. Nathan peeked out his bedroom door to see into the den where his father made his bed on the sofa.

Nate was still awake. The bed was made and his dad appeared ready for bed. He had no shoes or shirt on, but he was sitting on the sofa reading from a small book. Nathan had seen the book before. It was entitled *Christian Meditations for Recovery* and there was an entry for each day of the year.

Nate was reading now. Then he shut the book and bowed his head. He stayed like that for a few minutes. Nathan watched, amazed. He had never seen his father pray, other than the public prayers at church, and he wondered now if that was what Nate was doing.

His suspicions were confirmed when Nate made the sign of the Cross and then stretched out of the sofa. He was very still and seemed to go to sleep immediately; and Nathan had been sure he could now slip into the hall way and enter the kitchen quietly to place the box on the table. He looked toward the other end of the den and saw the door of the master bedroom firmly closed. His mother was already in her room, probably sleeping as well.

Kate had gone to bed earlier. She often went to bed early when she had to be at the hospital for the early shift. Nathan did not worry about her waking or hearing him return the box. He left his room without turning on the light and slipped into the kitchen.

When he set the box on the table, he realized that one of the articles had stuck to the outside of the box with old tape. Just setting the box down had jarred it loose and it went airborne for a minute before it coasted to a stop underneath the kitchen table.

Nathan got down on his hands and knees, still in the dark, to retrieve the loose article. Down there, on the floor, under the table, was where he was when he heard his mother's bedroom door open. He heard her footsteps moving to the den before he heard her say, "Nate, we need to talk."

His father must have been sleeping because it took a minute for him to respond, "Katie, Katie," he said, "What is it? Are you OK? Is Nathan OK?"

The lamp on the table clicked on and from his perch underneath the table, Nathan could see and hear both parents. It crossed his mind to make some noise, so they would know he was there, but he knew he would look stupid crawling out from underneath the table in the dark. He decided to wait it out. After all, he thought, he might learn something.

"We need to talk," Kate said again. Nathan could see that she was wearing her robe buttoned up to the neck and that she had on the fuzzy pink house shoes he had given her for Christmas. She sat down on the stool at the edge of the coffee table. She faced his father.

Nate was sitting up in his "bed" on the sofa, waiting for her to begin. He was without a shirt and Nathan noticed how well built his father had become. He must have worked out a lot in prison, Nathan thought. Muscles rippled when he moved.

"Here," Kate said to Nate, handing him his shirt, "Put on a shirt."

Nate slipped the shirt over his head and as it fell into place, he asked her again, "What is it? What is wrong?"

"I told you I would go to an Al-Anon Meeting," she began, "and I am going to go—to one. I just want to be sure that you understand that because I am going doesn't mean anything has changed between us," her voice trailed off.

"I am reminded that nothing has changed between us every night, Kate," Nate said, "every night that I sleep on this sofa!" Immediately Nate hated the sarcasm in his voice; maybe it was that he was just waking up, but the man he had become was struggling with the man he used to be. Nate knew it and thought about his hula hoop. He ran his hands thru his closely cropped hair and Nathan thought that he looked like he could have used a cigarette. He had not seen his father smoke since he returned home, but he thought he remembered that Nate used to smoke.

Katie ignored the sarcasm. "I mean, you seem to be doing well, and I am glad for you, Nate, I really am. Nathan seems to be adjusting well to having you back in his life . . . but understand, this is not your home. You have to find your own place as soon as you can."

Nathan could see his mother's face well, his father's, not so well. Kate was trying to be firm, Nathan could tell. Five years of just him and his mom, he thought he knew her well.

Nate did not say a word. He just waited. Then he spoke softly, "Go on."

Now it was Katie who ran her hands through her hair. Her hair was loose now and fell to shoulder length. Usually, she wore it tied back in a ponytail or twisted and fastened to the back of her head with a large clip, but now it was hanging loose. She brushed a strand away from her face. "Too much has happened, Nate. There was just too much time, this time. Nathan and I adjusted, we got our own place, we survived the Storm, we grew up as a family without you here," Kate paused. She had to go on, she had to get it said.

She continued. "Besides, I could just never trust you again. You had times before when you would do better for a while, then out of the blue, you would disappear for days and I would have no idea where you were, if you were coming back, or even if you wanted to come back. It was hell on earth. I don't want that again."

"I don't want that again either, Kate," Nate said. "I am sober now, I am working the Program. I am trying. I did terrible things when I was active in my addiction. I was not a good father to Nathan and I certainly was not a good husband to you. I cannot change that . . . God, if I had the power to change that I would." He looked distraught.

Nate continued, "I have to trust my Higher Power to stay sober each day. Sometimes that's hard, but I want it this time, Kate, and this time I have truly have had a Spiritual Awakening . . ."

"Do you mean you have gotten religion?" she asked. Nate could tell from her tone that "getting religion" was not a positive thing in her thinking.

"Addiction is a disease of the body and of the spirit," he said. "I don't think anyone can recover without the help of a High Power. I certainly cannot. My very best thinking just got me back in jail and back into my addiction. I had to have help from a Higher Power. My Higher Power is God, Jesus Christ. I believe that if I will give my life over to His guidance, He will direct me in the ways I should go, and He will keep me sober—one day at a time.

"Are you still Catholic?" Kate asked.

"I am Christian," he said. "I had my first communion at St. Anne's Church and I will continue to go there. Actually Father Sean knows a lot about recovery. I may go to services at other churches or denominations as well."

"You are really serious about all of this, aren't you, Nate?" she said. She was amazed.

"I have to be, Kate. In treatment we learned that an addiction leads to a mental hospital, a prison, or a cemetery—I've been in treatment for the mental illness of addiction, I've been to jail. My next stop, it's over."

"But, it's not just a "have to" thing with me now, Kate. I *want* to be sober, I *want* to serve and worship God. In a way I am thankful for my addiction. My counselor said we should welcome anything that brings us closer to our Higher Power. She is a Christian, she meant closer to Christ. Do you understand, Katie?"

"No," she said, shaking her head. "I feel like I am talking with somebody I don't even know."

"You know me, Katie," he said softly. He reached out his hand and placed it over Katie's hand. "I just want you to get to know who *you* are in recovery."

Kate pulled her hand away. "I am going to the meeting, Nate, because I told you I would. Just don't expect any big changes in my thinking. I am not trying to be mean, just honest."

Nate's mind went back to what he had learned in recovery. He had learned that honesty and tolerance were the two most important things families needed in early recovery. At least he and Kate were being honest. He told her that. "Thanks, Kate, for being so honest with me. I understand that you want me to find my own place. I have done some looking. I will have to be paid a couple of more times before I can move, but I promise you, I will not try to stay here if you don't want me here."

Nathan saw his mother pull her robe tightly around her and stand up. "Thank you, Nate," she said before she turned and walked into her bedroom again.

His father got up then and walked to the window. He put his hand near to top of the window frame and learned on the window sill looking into the complete blackness of the night. Nate dropped his head and continued to stand there without seeing Nathan when he slipped back into his room.

CHAPTER 20

Kate went to work early the next morning and Nathan got up early to go with the youth group at church to an overnight retreat. They were leaving on Saturday morning and planning to return in time for the later mass on Sunday. It would be the first time Nate and Kate had stayed alone in the house since his return. After her conversation the night before, Nate was dreading the time alone with her.

He locked the house on his way out and decided to take a walk. It was early still and cooler than usual for a summer day in New Orleans. Nate walked through the park, past the church, and on to the old high school. It was the middle school now, the school Nathan attended.

The playing fields were still there and soon his stroll led him to the baseball field. It was empty so early in the day and he walked past the fading dugouts to the center of the field. Nate took the mound.

He stood there, looking up into the stands. Katie usually sat about half way up on the third base line. Nate could almost see her there in his imagination. He could almost hear her encouragement, "One more, Nate," or "He can't hit you—don't worry about it, we've got your back."

Nate dropped his head. He left the mound and walked over to the dug out and sat down. So much had happened since he had stood on that mound, he thought, as he looked back at it now.

He had started chasing that first high from cocaine, he thought. It was never like the first time, never. But that had not stopped him from trying.

Nate thought more about that high. I wonder how long a person has to stay off the drug to get that high again? His thinking was familiar now. I wonder if five years off the drug would give the effect of the first time, he thought.

Nate looked toward the street. He could go back up the street, past the church, back to the life he had started now—the life with or without Katie. Or, he could go down the street . . .

Nate checked his pockets. He had thirty-two dollars in his jeans. It would take less than ten minutes to get the drug, and less time than that to use it. Then he would know about the effect after so much time without use. Who would really care? he asked himself. Certainly not Kate.

I would only do it once, Nate thought. Kate and Nathan would never know. Not even his sponsor would know. Nate would be careful, he was, after all, smarter than most, he thought.

Higher Power? Yeah, He would know, but wouldn't He understand? God was in the forgiving business, he could ask for forgiveness again, couldn't he? He could make it right again with his Higher Power, or could he?

Hating himself already, Nate got up from the dugout and resigned himself to his decision. As he left the school, he heard the voices of children playing in the yard across the street. He looked up to watch the children and saw that one of them was playing with a hula hoop.

Nate remembered a hula hoop saying from his days in treatment. "Why would someone who believes he has been rescued from hell ever *choose* to go back?"

He stood at the edge of the street—up or down? He had to decide now. He had to decide for today. Nate choose not to go back. He turned to walk back up the street, past the church, back to the life he was choosing today.

He took the cell phone from his pocket. Nate called his sponsor. "I need to talk with you and I need a meeting," he said, "now!"

CHAPTER 21

"Come on over and let me introduce you to the boys," Justin said to Nate. It was the first time Nate had come to practice and he was surprised to realize how nervous he felt meeting a group of eleven and twelve year olds.

"This is Nathan's father," Justin said. "He is going to be one of our pitching coaches, our main pitching coach." Justin remembered that Nate had asked that he not talk about his high school honors and said simply, "He know a little bit about throwing a baseball."

There were four pitchers there, Nathan among them. They seemed shy and he felt shy, but Nate forced himself to speak. "Let's see what you've got," he said, throwing out the balls. All at once, pitches were flying. The sound of leather popping filled the air with each pitch. Nate was surprised how quickly it all came back to him. It was immediately obvious to Nate that Nathan and another kid named Keith were the best on the team. He wondered if that would be good or bad.

He decided to take them two at a time, watching mostly, but making a few simple suggestions. "Watch the zone first, then speed. Not too much, Save the arm." He felt Nathan's eyes on him when he spoke.

Nate stopped the group after a while addressed each boy's wind up. He tried to analyze how it could be improved to get technique well-established from the very beginning. Speed and power could come much later, when their bodies were bigger and stronger.

When practice was over and Nate was gathering up the baseballs from the field, Nathan honored him by joining him. "Would you like to buy me and Mindy some ice cream?" he asked Nate. Nate looked over toward the scoreboard and saw Mindy sitting atop a dirt hill behind the fence. He had not even known that she was there. "She do that often?" he asked Nathan.

"All the time," Nathan said.

"Do you mind?" Nate asked.

"Why would I mind?" Nathan replied. "It's just Mindy."

"Go get her and tell her I am buying ice cream," Nathan said.

It took only a minute for Mindy to join them. "Hi, Mr. Matthews," she said shyly. Then, "don't you think Nathan is a great pitcher?"

Nathan groaned.

"He's OK," Nate said. "He just needs to eat more ice cream. Would you like to go with us to get ice cream?"

"Will I be home by street lights?" she asked

"Absolutely," Nate said.

"I can't make my dad mad. He's been mad at my brother, Jake, a lot lately and I can't make him mad."

"He's never mad at you," Nathan said. "Dad, her dad is never mad at her. He doesn't think she ever does anything wrong."

"Do you?" Nate asked laughing.

""Nope," she said. Then, "I mean, no, sir. It's Jake who makes him mad. It is like he tries to!"

"Well, don't worry. You will be home in plenty of time," Nate said. They were entering the ice cream shop.

"There's Jake now," Mindy said.

Nate took in the scene. Jake was dressed in a style admirable to the street. His pants were low on his thin hips and he had a large, loose shirt out over his jeans. He walked with a swagger and he stood in deep conversation with another young man. He quickly surmised that Jake was trouble, or about to be in trouble. He made a mental note to ask Kate if Nathan spent any time with this kid.

"Hi, Jake," Mindy said. Her smile was sweet and when Jake turned to the sound of her voice his face softened for a moment as he looked at his little sister.

"Kid," he said. Then, "Hey, Nathan, S'up?"

"Not much" Nathan said. "This is my dad."

Jake's eyes widened in surprise. Nate knew that Jake must know where he had been and that Jake was disappointed that Nate did not have the look of a criminal, but rather just looked like any other dad who had been at work all day and was now taking his kid to an ice cream shop. Nate liked disappointing people in that way.

Looking into Jake's eyes at closer range was like looking back into his own history. Jake was high and he smelled like he had been smoking weed. A quick look at Mindy and Nathan made Nate aware that they saw nothing unusual about Jake. That could mean they did not realize he was high or it could mean that Jake was usually high and they had come to expect it. Nate would bet that both Mindy and Nathan knew.

"Would you like some ice cream, Jake?" Nate asked. Why couldn't life just be simple. Why couldn't Jake just join them for ice cream?

CHAPTER 22

Nate and Kate walked up the brick steps that led to the doorway at the side entrance of the old church building. A light was on down the hall and the smell of coffee perking was in the air. Voices could be heard even before they entered the room.

"Hi, Nate," Ms. Ellen said. She was a middle-aged lady with a friendly smile and she was a regular at the Al-Anon meetings at the church. "This must be your wife, Kate. Right?"

Nate stumbled over identifying Kate as his wife. Actually she *was* technically his wife. They were not divorced *yet*. Katie was watching now, he knew, to gauge his response. He answered safely, "This is Kate."

"Welcome to the group," Ms. Ellen said. "Is this your first meeting?"

Kate was nervous, not knowing what to expect. "Yes," she said, "my first." The look that she gave to Nate let him know that she wanted to add, "and my last," but being polite prevented.

"We meet each week at the same time the AA's, and CA's do,"—meaning Alcoholic Anonymous and Cocaine Anonymous members. She continued, "Once a month, we have a joint meeting. I am so glad you decided to come. Nate has become a regular since he has been at home."

So they knew Nate's history, Kate thought. That meant they knew her history as well. She did not like the idea of anyone knowing her business. What happened in a family needed to stay in the family—that is what she had been taught. Even when Nate was using heavily, *active in his addiction* as he liked to say now, she had only spoken about it when she *had* to speak of it—like when she had to ask her parents for money, or when she had to miss work or school to go out and try to find him. Already she was feeling resistant to the meeting that was about to happen here.

More people came into the room. Some came alone. They were friendly and seemed not to judge anyone. Almost everyone was drinking coffee. When the clock said 7:00 P.M., the group divided. Those who were alcoholics and addicts went into one room and those who were there for Al-Anon went into another.

There were seven in Kate's group—Ms. Ellen, a couple in their fifties, another young woman in her thirties, a couple in their twenties who said they were brother and sister, and Kate. Kate looked around the room. A poster on the wall read, "The Three C's of Addiction: You did not *cause* it, you cannot *cure* it, but you can *cope* with it." Can I *cope* with it? thought Kate. Can I *cope* with Nate's returning home?

On the opposing wall was a copy of the Serenity Prayer and that was how the meeting began. Ms. Ellen said, "Let's begin with a moment of silence followed by the Serenity Prayer.

The group bowed its head. When she spoke the word, "God," the group began, "God, grant me the serenity to accept the things I cannot change, the courage to change the things I can, and the wisdom to know the difference."

Ms. Ellen began reading the opening: "The Al-Anon Family Groups are a fellowship of relatives and friends of alcoholics (addicts) who share their experience, strength and hope in order to solve their common problems. We believe alcoholism is a family illness and that changed attitudes can aid recovery."

Kate's mind began to wander a bit while Ms. Ellen continued reading. She tuned in again for the final sentences. "Al-Anon has but one purpose: to help families of alcoholics (addicts). We do this by practicing the Twelve Steps, by welcoming and giving comfort to families of addicts, and by giving understanding and encouragement to the alcoholic/addict."

After the opening, Ms. Ellen introduced Kate. "This is a newcomer, Nate's wife, Kate," she said. Apparently Ms. Ellen had no difficulty identifying her as Nate's wife.

"Actually, Nate is just staying with Nathan, our son, and me until he can find a place of his own," Kate explained and was instantly sorrow that she had done so. She wondered why she had felt comfortable saying this to strangers. Already the group was making her feel comfortable and safe and she was feeling the need to talk openly. *I don't think* so. She told herself silently. She checked herself and grew quiet.

The young woman, whose name was Rose, completed a reading from *Once Day at a Time in Al-Anon*. The reading quoted someone who said that in her early days of dealing with her husband's addiction, she had rejected God because she was angry and considered her marriage to an addict "unfair punishment" to have her life aligned with someone suffering an addiction. Then later, the reading said, the author, in desperation, had turned to God again and placed her life in His hands. Then as Dante wrote in Divine comedy, she found that "In His will is our peace."

Why that made Kate want to cry, she did not know. She turned her attention to the man in the couple. He was saying, "Our son is active in his addiction now. He uses drugs, sells drugs, has been to jail and will likely go back to jail. We are afraid every night that we will get a call telling us he has died in his addiction. His mother and I would be insane if we did not the fellowship of those in the program, the help that being with others who understand provides.

Kate did feel comforted, but was still quite unwilling to let Nate know she was finding some solace in the words being shared in the room. When they left the meeting that night, Kate was quiet. Nate suggested that they stop for ice cream on the way home. As they sat together in the dainty chairs of the ice cream parlor, Kate looked carefully at Nate. Was it possible that she had been ill as well as he? She decided that she would go to a few more meetings. Maybe that would help her realize that she was *not* a part of the problem and that she had just been unfortunate in marrying an addict. Yes, she would go back.

———————

Kate had been attending Al-Anon meetings for three weeks now. Things seemed to be going well at home. Nate and Nathan were focused on ball practice and preparing for the upcoming game. As if practice was not enough, it was not uncommon to see

Nathan pitching baseballs into Nate's heavy catcher's mitt, when she came home after working until noon on Saturdays.

Nate was giving advice, "Use your legs, Nathan. You should be dropping your knee. You get power from your legs." Nathan instantly corrected and they two of them looked as if they had never lost a day as father and son.

Even though she had attended a number of meetings, Kate was still not ready to accept that she might have a problem too. At each meeting, she listened intently, but did not speak at all. Tonight Ms. Ellen was going to tell her Al-Anon story. Kate was interested to hear what she might say, and she told Nate on the way to the meeting that she was going to hear one of the "old timers" tell her story tonight.

"Ah," Nate replied. "Ms. Ellen is going to talk. She told her story at the last joint meeting before you started coming. It is amazing."

"I haven't *started* coming, Nate," Kate corrected, although this would be her seventh meeting. "Don't think this is going to be a habit with me. I just am interested in hearing what some of them have to say."

"OK," Nate said, as they entered the building.

Ms. Ellen opened the meeting in the usual way. After the brief reading, Ms. Ellen began to speak and Kate felt as if she were talking just to her. "When my husband was an active alcoholic, I used to hate the drinking the same way I would have hated another woman in my husband's life. I followed him around, I accused him of going out just to drink, I was jealous, angry-raging, in fact. I used to wish it were another woman instead of the alcohol. Then, I would at least have an enemy to fight. But I felt I was competing with a liquid—a liquid!" Everyone laughed. "How do you compete with a liquid?" She asked.

"Finally, I realized that Don was sick. He was sick and I was sick, too. I may have been sicker that he was. I was trying to control him and his addiction, and I couldn't even control me! I felt self-righteous, like a martyr for staying in my marriage. I had to get better . . . I had become someone I did not like at all. When I came to Al-Anon, I was angry and resentful and I stayed that way for several months before the program made any sense to me. Now I thank God, my Higher Power, for it every day."

How could this woman know just what Kate felt? Nate's drugs and alcohol had felt like competition to her. She could not have been any more angry if she had found him with someone else. She heard herself start to talk, "I wanted to be close to Nate. I wanted him to turn to me when he had a problem or when he felt afraid or unsure. I even wanted him to share his joys with me. Nate shared every emotion that he had with his drugging friends, and later when he got worse, he shared everything with the drugs alone. He didn't go out or even want to go out. He never used at home, because of Nathan, I think, but he mostly used alone. I would find him in a cheap hotel, or the backroom of some apartment—an abandoned building. Then I quit looking for him. I couldn't take a baby out into the night to look for its father. I just waited to see if he would come home of if the cops would come to tell me he was dead."

"When he would come home after days of being loaded," she continued, "I would be so glad to see him, so relieved that he was alive, but all I could do or say was something mean and hateful. Nate doesn't know, but I knew deep inside of me that there were other women. I told him he didn't love me or Nathan." Tears started to slip from Kate's eyes as she continued talking. "I didn't know he was sick. Sometimes, he would promise me he would quit, and everything would be great for a while, then he would disappear again. I didn't want my parents to know, but I had to tell them finally. I had to have their help.

Nate was spending all our money, stealing, robbing. He was someone I did not even recognize! My parents hated him—still do! My mom is still alive and she hates Nate. Nobody believes he will stay sober. *I* don't even believe it and I hope Nathan doesn't. Nate has been home almost five weeks now and I am still mad at him! I am mad at him for leaving me alone for the past five years while he was in prison. I am mad at him for ruining the fairytale romance we had. I am just so mad!" Kate was actually clenching her fists.

"Would you be mad at him if he had another disease like cancer or diabetes?" Rose asked.

"What?" Katie said, not understanding, "What?"

"Another disease—if he had cancer, would you be made at him? Would you think that the love you had for each other would cure it?"

"Of course not," Kate said. She looked around the room to each person, trying to digest what Rose was saying and wondering if she were the only one having trouble.

It was the mother of the young addict who was still 'out there' who spoke, "Addiction is a disease. They cannot stop. Their lives are unmanageable. The addict has to accept that and realize that a Power greater than himself can restore him to sanity and he has to turn his life over to that Power. That's how addicts recover."

"That's how addicts recover," Ms. Ellen said, "and that is how we recover. We work the Twelve Steps and we pray for wisdom to apply them in our everyday lives. We, too, do it one day at a time."

"That's all the time we have tonight," Ms. Ellen said. "Kate, thank you for sharing and please keep coming back. The Program does "work if you work it!" We usually end with the Lord's Prayer.

The members of the group stood and joined hands. Heads bowed, they repeated together, "Our Father, Who are in heaven, Hallowed be Thy name. Thy kingdom come, Thy will be done, on earth as it is in heaven. Give us this day, our daily bread, and forgive us our trespasses as we forgive those who trespass against us. And lead us not into temptation, but deliver us from evil, for Thine is the kingdom, and the power, and the glory forever, Amen

CHAPTER 23

It was a starry night in New Orleans. The moon was full and hanging just over the cypress trees when Nate and Kate left the church after their Meetings. Nate wanted to take Katie's hand for the stroll home in the moonlight, but it was still too early. *Too early,* he thought. *That was being optimistic. He may never take Katie's hand again.*

She had not said a word as they were leaving the building. Nate really could not read her mood. He could tell that she was upset, but beyond that, he had no idea what she was thinking. He was afraid that something in the Meeting had upset her and that this would be her last time to go. Already, he could see changes in her that he knew had come from changes in thinking that she was learning in the program. Nate really did not want her to give up now, not when he felt they were so close to reaching an understanding about his addiction and what it had cost their family.

Nate wanted Katie to find the recovery that he had found. He did not want this for himself, but for her. He knew that Katie was a spiritual person. She had been diligent about taking Nathan to church, always seeing that he attended classes and events to give him a foundation of faith. Nate wanted Katie to reconnect to her Higher Power, to know the peace that he now knew.

There had been a time in their lives when Katie had been very active in their youth group at St. Anne's. She was musical, played piano, the organ, keyboard. When they were in high school, she had often played for services at St. Anne's.

Katie used to talk a lot about doing something in her life to help people. That is why she had chosen nursing as a profession, and Nate knew now, why she had chosen him as a husband.

There had been youth retreats when they were in high school, times of special focus on religious callings. Kate had admitted to the priest that she thought she may have been called for some special service. Katie thought that, and then there had been his addiction, Nate reminded himself.

Nate knew that his addiction had robbed them both of many of their dreams. He stayed focused on his drugs and Katie stayed focused on changing him. It had been miserable for them both, with only a few moments of joy dispersed along the way. Nathan's birth's had given them hope as a couple, but it did not take long for even that to be clouded by his addiction.

Nate remembered that when he was in his addiction he had lied to everyone he knew, especially to Katie. He could not stop using the drugs or drinking. He did not understand why he could not stop. He had really meant it each time he had told her he had used his last drug, drunk his last beer. He meant it this time, and still, all he could promise her, even now, was one day at a time.

The difference now was his relationship with Jesus Christ. Nate believed with all his heart that as long as he asked Christ on a daily basis to guide his steps, he would stay sober. He believed it, but he had no idea how to communicate that to his wife, especially when he had lied to her so often in the past.

He looked at her now, walking beside him. The moonlight shone on her pale red hair. Her green eyes looked up to him. "What?" she asked.

"Nothing," he said, "nothing," and they just kept walking.

When they arrived home, Nathan was talking on the phone. He turned to them. "Is it all right if Mindy comes over and watches a movie? Her dad says she can if you guys are at home and if she calls him to pick her up when it is over."

"What movie?" Kate asked, uttering her first words since ordering pizza on the way home from the meeting.

"It's a kid move," Nathan said, almost apologetically, "but Mindy wants to watch it. *The Chronicles of Narnia.*"

"That's a great movie," Nate said. "A lot of symbolism in it. Have you read the books?"

"Yes sir, we had to read them in school," Nathan said.

"It's fine," Kate said. "Do we need to pick her up?"

"No, her dad is bringing her."

Katie put the pizza on the table and called Nathan to join them. Nate was pouring soda in glasses. The family sat down to eat and Nate and Nathan devoured pieces of pizza quickly. Kate ate nothing.

"Aren't you hungry, Katie?" Nate asked. He was feeling more tender and protective of her than usual for some reason.

"Not really," she said. "Go ahead." She sat silently at the table while they finished the pizza and put the plates in the dishwasher. She was still sitting there when Mindy knocked at the door.

Nate went to the door and Mindy and her father stepped inside. The men shook hands and Nate assured Mindy's dad that he and Kate would be at home and they would see that Mindy called him when the movie was done. Nathan and Mindy disappeared into Nathan's room with the DVD in hand.

"Leave the door open," Nate said.

"What?" Nathan asked.

"Leave the door open," Nate repeated.

"Why?" Nathan asked again.

"Leave it open," Nate said without further explanation.

"All right," Nathan said and he entered his room shaking his head.

The musical score from the movie started, signaling its beginning and Nate returned to the kitchen table where Kate had been sitting all this time. Her head was lowered and she appeared to be staring at the table. "Kate," he asked her, "is something wrong?"

"I had no idea," she said to the table. Then she looked up. Her eyes were swimming, but not yet overflowing when she looked at Nate. She began slowly, "Nate, I had no idea . . ."

"No idea about what?" he asked, thinking that he knew, but needing her to express herself clearly.

"I had no idea it was *really* is a disease. I thought that calling it a disease was just a way to soften what I thought you had done to us. I mean, you hear it all the time, *a disease*. Everyone does. But it *really* is an illness. You can inherit the tendency for it from your parents," she said. She stopped then and took a deep breath.

That troublesome strand of hair was falling into her face again and hid her eyes. "I've been thinking about your dad, how things were with him when we were younger," she looked up. "You have been suffering from the disease of addiction in one way or another for your entire life! You got this disease from your father, from your family before him. It really is a disease, a *family* disease and we have it, Nate. Our *family* has this disease! It affects all of us."

Nate could have said a lot, but he was learning to be silent and let others form their own conclusions. He simply reached up to gently brush her hair from her face. When he did he could see that the tears had begun to escape their boundaries. When she met his gaze, they were flowing silently down her face.

"I am so sorry, Nate. So sorry for not understanding, for not *trying* to understand. I did not know I was a part of this. I did not know my attitudes and behaviors contributed to the disease," she said to him.

Nate had waited a very long time to hear those words. He had prayed diligently in his cell at night that whether he and Katie were able to restore their marriage and make it as a couple or not, that she would come to understand. His using drugs and drinking had not been because he had failed to love her or failed to love Nathan; it had been because he was sick. He was responsible for the bad decisions he had made to support his illness, but it *was* an illness and now Katie knew that. He thanked God for his answered prayer and felt his own eyes filling with tears. All he could think of to say when she looked back at him was, "I love you, Katie."

CHAPTER 24

When Nathan and Mindy finished watching the *Chronicles of Narnia*, she called her dad and he came immediately to pick her up. Nathan had sat at the kitchen table with her until her dad arrived, but when she left he went into the den where his parents were sitting and talking. They were both on the sofa and they seemed to be in a very serious conversation.

Nathan was surprised to see that the television was not even on. The stereo was softly playing some 80's music. His parents seemed so intense that he wondered if he were in trouble. He thought about the day and could think of nothing he had done wrong lately.

"Do we have practice tomorrow, Dad?" he asked. The team was getting ready for the all-city tournament.

"Five o'clock," Nate said, "same field."

"I'm tired, I am going to bed," Nathan said. He kissed his mom goodnight and went into his room and shut the door. When

Nate eased the door open ten minutes later, Nathan was already sleeping soundly.

Nathan was awakened suddenly by a loud banging at the door. The doorbell was ringing frantically and someone was continuing to pound on the door. He jumped from his bed and opened the door to the hallway.

He saw light from his mother's open bedroom door. His parents looked as if they had been asleep for several hours and his father was hurriedly pulling on his jeans and heading to the door. His mother was following. "Who is it, Nate? What's wrong?"

Nathan had made it to the kitchen when Nate opened the door. He looked up and then down to see Mindy's face. She was crying hysterically. "My dad and my brother are fighting!" she said.

Nathan pushed his way in front of his father to stand before Mindy just as his mother said. "What? What happened, Mindy?"

"My dad and my brother—they are fighting!"

"Are they still fighting?" Nate asked, ready to leave suddenly if he had to go.

"No, not when I left," she said between sobs. "But they were very mad—both of them."

"Was Jake high?" Nathan asked her and Nate registered that, indeed, both Nathan and Mindy knew that Jake was using drugs.

"Yes," she said. "Jake came home late, later than his curfew and Dad was mad. Dad could tell he was high and they started arguing about Jake's friends and that's when they started fighting."

Nate was looking for his shoes and a shirt, still preparing to go with Mindy if he needed. "What exactly happened in the fight, Mindy?" he asked.

Kate had set a glass of water in front of Mindy and was sitting at the table with her arm protectively around Mindy's shoulder. Mindy breathed deeply and started to speak, "My dad told my brother that he knew he was high. He told him that he did not like the friends he was keeping. Jake told him he didn't care if he liked them or not—and then Jake hit my dad!"

"What did your dad do?" Nate asked. "Did he hit him back? He is a lot bigger than your brother." Nate exchanged a look with Katie. The memory of similar scenes with his own father was returning.

"Not really," she said. "Dad just mostly tried to stop Jake from hitting him. Dad was really mad, but he didn't hit Jake. He wrestled Jake to the floor and held him there until Jake quit trying to hit him."

Nate breathed more easily. "Call her dad, Katie," he said. "Tell him she is here."

"Yes," Katie said into the phone. "She is here, she is with us. She is fine. She was a bit upset, but she is OK now. Why don't you let her stay here for the night? She can sleep here and you can pick her up in the morning. It's very late and everyone needs to get to sleep."

Katie nodded to Nate. "It's OK if you stay here, Mindy. Let's make a bed for you on the sofa." Katie moved into the den to help Mindy make her bed.

Nathan looked in the den. The sofa where his dad had been sleeping since his return still had the sheets and blankets folded neatly on the table nearby. That was when it registered with Nathan that his dad and mom had come out of the same room when Mindy knocked at the door.

Nate had been watching him, watching him as he put the pieces together and drew the correct conclusion. Nathan looked at him and grinned. "I am really not as dumb as you think I am," Nathan said.

"Go to bed," Nate said, "and mind your own business." He put a fatherly hand on Nathan's head and gave his already tousled hair a rub.

CHAPTER 25

Katie made pancakes the next morning and Nathan and Mindy were just finishing breakfast when Mindy's father arrived to take her home. Nate stepped outside the door to talk with him alone.

"Thanks so much, Ms. Matthews," Mindy said. "I am sorry I woke you up."

"You can do that anytime you need, Sweetie," Katie said. She planted a kiss on top of Mindy's head. Nathan had not seen his mother seem so happy in a long time, he thought.

"Thanks again," Mindy's dad was saying to Nate. They shook hands.

"Anyway we can help," Nate assured him and then returned inside. "I've got to fix a sandwich for lunch," he said, opening the refrigerator, searching.

"Here," Katie said as she placed his already packed lunch box on the counter. "I did it already." It reminded Nate of early marriage. Then Katie packed his lunch every day and usually put a note saying 'I love you' inside. He wondered if he had a note today.

Nate looked at Nathan. "Her brother selling drugs?" he asked him, pouring another glass of milk.

"I don't know," Nathan said.

"Yes, you do," Nate said. "You may not want to tell me, but you know." Nate was not angry, but he felt it was important that Nathan realize now that fooling him, especially about things such as this, was going to be difficult. Nathan's eyes went to the floor, confirming what Nate had already strongly suspected.

"Is he using too?" Nate asked.

"Maybe a little," Nathan said.

"What?"

"Weed, mostly. Some Ex pills . . ."

"Cocaine?"

"I think he has tried it," Nathan said. He looked sad. "It really upsets Mindy."

"I am sure it does," Katie replied.

"I am sure he drinks, too," Nate said. "Does Mindy's father drink?" Nate knew he had smelled alcohol the night before when Mindy was dropped off to watch the movie.

"He drinks, but he is not an alcoholic," Nathan answered. "He doesn't drink every day and he never drinks in the morning. He never drinks when he is working. He just drinks on weekends—sometimes he gets drunk, but he is not an alcoholic."

"A person does not have to drink every day to be an alcoholic," Nate said. "A lot of people are confused about that. You can be an episodic drinker, someone who drinks every few days or even every few months. They are people who are unable to stop their drinking before getting drunk. One of my counselors said that she asks people if they are drinking for relief. She thinks that anyone who is using alcohol or drugs to get relief from their feelings is an alcoholic or at least a potential alcoholic. A lot of other professionals agree with her."

Katie shook her head. "That's a real shame for that family. I am so sorry Mindy is having to live with that and deal with it at such a young age."

Nate looked at the clock. "I've got to run," he said and put his arms around Katie who was standing at the sink. He bent to kiss her good-bye.

"Nate!" she said and pulled away. She motioned her head toward Nathan who was in plain view at the table.

"Oh, him" Nate said, attempting to kiss her again. "He knows."

"I know," Nathan said grinning at his mom as he grabbed his ball cap and went out the door before his father. "I have to go," he said. "I promised Father Sean I would help with the sports for the little kids at summer church camp today."

Nate stayed inside only long enough to accomplish his purpose with Katie and then joined his son on the walk. Katie watched them walk away together. They were talking and laughing as they walked down the street. Nate put his hand on Nathan's shoulder as they parted ways at the corner. Life was finally getting better, she thought.

CHAPTER 26

Today's practice was an important one. It was the last before the beginning of the all-city play-offs. The team would play for a position in the tournament. They played the opening team twice. If they won both, they did not have to play again until the start of the tournament in two weeks. If they lost, they had to play a team from the other side of the city. They needed to win.

Nate thought about who he would start on the mound. Nathan was by far the strongest pitcher on the team. The next, a kid named Keith, was better than average, but not nearly the natural athlete that Nathan was. Nate had a sense of humility about it, but he realized that Nathan had probably inherited much of his athletic abilities from him.

Everything about throwing a baseball came easily to Nathan. He had a natural instinct that made him use his whole body in the way that he should to get maximum effect. All he was going to need to be a great high school athlete, and maybe more, was more strength and a continued good attitude. Nathan had a heart for the win and that was a tremendous asset.

Keith, Nate had observed, was a bit of a bully. He was always picking on the smaller kids. He was a little heavy, but still agile. And, Nate admitted, he appeared to be someone who could benefit from coaching. He tried to do whatever Nate asked of him, but sometimes he just did not get it.

Nate was unsure who to start. His instincts told him to start Nathan and intimidate the opponent, but he wanted to be fair. He did not want the other kids or the parents to think that he was putting his kid out in front. He would probably start Keith. Maybe if the kid got a little glory with a win, it would help his attitude.

Practice went well. The fielders were hitting above average. He watched Justin pitching to the kids who were practicing hitting. Nate almost laughed. Justin could not pitch has way out of a paper bag! Justin had been a catcher. He was a year older than Nate, but he had caught him a few times Nate's junior year.

Practice was ending when one of the kids said, "Pitch for us, Mr. Nate." Despite his efforts to keep it quiet, they had heard about his high school career, and mercifully Nate had learned that his sports history mattered more to the kids on the team than his criminal history.

"Nahh," Nate said, gathering equipment.

"Come on, please," another said. And then, there was a chorus of twelve year olds begging their one agenda. They wanted to see Nate pitch.

"No," Nate said.

"Why not?" Justin said. "I'll catch you. It will be like old times."

"Why?" Nathan asked him. It was then that he heard the familiar voice. "Come on, Dad, just a few."

He looked at Nathan. "OK," he agreed. "Just a few."

There had been softball in prison, but it had been years since Nate had stood on a pitcher's mound with a baseball in his hand. The boys stood along side each baseline as Justin went into the dugout for a better catcher's mitt.

The first ball went right to the center of the strike zone. It moved accurately, but without the speed that Justin remembered.

"Come on, Nate, one just like against St. Al's," Justin said.

This time the ball moved with greater force. It popped into the leather mitt making a sound that separated it from the earlier sounds of Dixie Youth Baseball.

Suddenly, time opened up. Nate was seventeen again and all he could see was the signal from Justin and the waiting glove. He went into his wind up and released the ball perfectly. It bore down on the center of the strike zone with tremendous speed. Then, at the last moment, dropped to capture only a small corner of the plate.

"Wow!"

"Boy, Mr. Nate, you can really throw!"

"I didn't know your dad could do that, Nathan."

Nate returned to reality. The muscles in his back and legs were already letting him know that perhaps this had not been a good idea.

The Kids were excited though. They were jumping around, talking loudly, having a good time—all except for Keith. He appeared to be pouting.

When the equipment was stored and everyone was leaving the field, Nate noticed that Keith was still sitting in the empty stands. As he and Nathan walked toward the playground, Nate asked, "Tell me about Keith. What does his dad do?"

"He doesn't have a dad. I mean, his dad left when he was a baby. I think he lives in Minnesota, but Keith does not even hear from him at Christmastime, Nathan said. "I know I should feel sorry for him, but I don't. He is a jerk."

"What do you mean?" Nate asked.

"He's always picking on people, usually someone younger or smaller—always fighting."

"Does he pick on you?" Nate asked.

"No, I would not stand for that," Nathan said.

"I don't have much use for fighting," Nate warned, thinking, 'not anymore,' but not saying it.

"I don't either, Dad," Nathan replied. "I wonder what Mom is cooking."

Apparently the conversation was over, Nate realized.

CHAPTER 27

"You knew that I would have to talk with her," Nate told Katie. They were discussing her mother, the woman they all called, 'Nana.' Katie did know. After a few more weeks at Al-Anon, she understood that part of the recovery program included contacting those people who had been hurt by your addictive behaviors and trying to make amends to them. Her mother had to be high on Nate's list.

Before he went to prison, Nate knew that Katie's parents had encouraged her to "get him out of her life." They were actually relieved when the state did the job for her. They were glad that he got five years without chance of parole or "good time credit," a means to earn some time subtracted from the sentence. Ten years would have been better than five!

He could not really blame them. They had given him every chance in the world, and he had blown all of them. Even when he and Katie were in high school, they had been kind to him. It was only when his addictive behaviors began to take him over that they

120

had come to despise him. Nate's only saving grace with Nana was that he had fathered Nathan and Nathan was her heart.

Katie's dad had died while Nate was in prison. He had been killed in a single vehicle accident on his way home from a night at the country club where he had celebrated with friends after winning a golf tournament. Nate knew that his drinking had likely contributed to his death. Only now, with some recovery in Al-Anon, could Katie admit that her dad had been a functional alcoholic.

Nana had chosen to live on in her home in Covington. Fortunately, it had been untouched by the Storm and not much in her life had been forced to change. She still stayed in daily touch with her daughter and complained when Katie and Nathan were "too busy" to visit.

"Do you want me to go with you?" Katie asked. She knew that Nate had called Nana and asked to take her to lunch.

"Do you think I need protecting?" Nate asked.

"No . . ." Katie replied. "I *know* you are going to need protecting!" Katie was operating under no illusions that Nana would be glad to see him.

"I will be fine," Nate replied.

Katie dropped him off at the restaurant and left to do some shopping. Nate went inside and found Nana waiting—she was early. They ordered lunch. Nana ordered a glass of wine.

After a polite question or two about Nathan's baseball team, Nana looked at Nate squarely. "Why did you want to see me?" she asked.

"Nana," Nate began. "I have been sober almost six years—nearly two months if you want to start counting when I got home. I am working the Twelve Step program and one of the things I have to do—one of the things I *want* to do—is tell you how sorry I am for the problems that I caused for you while I was using drugs and drinking. I lied to you. I lied to Katie. I stole money and things from you. I probably do not remember all the things I did that hurt you, but mainly I hurt Katie. I know how I would feel if someone were hurting Nathan and I could do nothing about it. I would be very slow to forgive them, but I have to ask for your forgiveness and tell you I hope to work my program every day and stay sober for myself and for Katie and Nathan." He stopped to breathe.

Nana continued to look at him. She was not making this easy and Nate knew she enjoyed his discomfort. Finally she spoke.

"Nate, Katie has loved you since she was ten years old. It made me sick to see what you did to her. It's going to take a very long time before I can even think about trusting you again," she said. The look that she gave him could only be given by an older, determined lady.

"I know," he said. Nate felt fourteen, but it had to be done. 'I am sorry that I was unable to talk to her dad. I am sorry, Nana, for your loss. He was a good man."

He had been a good man, Nate thought. Nate had no doubt that Katie's father had been an alcoholic, but he had been a wonderful man. He was a good provider and he loved his family. Katie was his only child and he adored her. He adored Nathan. Nathan's grandfather had really stepped up when Nate had been taken away.

"I can't change any of it, Nana," Nate said. "I wish I could. I just want you to know I am sorry and that I hope some day you can forgive me."

"I hope I can, too, Nate. We will just have to see what happens *this* time, won't we?" she said and took another sip of wine.

CHAPTER 28

Thunder and lightning were crashing outside when Nate woke early on a Saturday morning. He heard the rain and knew there would be no ball practice today. Katie did not have to work today and she was sleeping beside him now in the new king-sized bed they had purchased just last week. Nate was much more comfortable in the larger bed. Katie stirred beside him, opened her eyes, and smiled.

Just as Nate turned toward her, the bedroom door burst open and Nathan plopped onto the end of the bed. "Boy, did you hear that thunder?" he said. "It woke me up!"

"So nice to see you, son," Nate said, sitting up in bed.

Katie leveled him with a look before saying, "I'll make some coffee." She left the room and when she returned ten minutes later, Nate and Nathan were already talking about baseball. She handed Nate a cup of coffee and handed Nathan a bottle of chocolate milk.

"Can't you two talk about anything but baseball?" she said as she got back into bed with her own cup of coffee. The rain continued even louder.

"What do you want us to talk about, Mom?" Nathan asked.

"Why don't we talk about prison?" Nate said.

Both Nathan and Katie looked at him in surprise.

"You know it is a part of my life," Nate said. "Sometimes I feel like it is just hanging over us and we need to talk about it. Is there anything you'd like to know about? Anything you want to ask me?" he said.

There were a lot of things that Nathan wanted to know about his father. He had plenty of questions. Nathan looked at his mother. She had no emotion that he could read so he continued on his own.

"Dad, were you safe in prison?" Nathan asked.

"I'm not sure what you mean, Nathan. No one is safe in prison," he replied, but could tell he had not answered adequately by the quizzical look still on Nathan's face. Then he understood the question.

"You mean, was I assaulted, assaulted in prison like you see on the movies?" Nate said. "No, never," he explained. Nate heard Katie exhale and realized she had been holding her breath, waiting to hear his response also. She had been wondering about it as well and he wondered why she had not just asked him.

Nate took Katie's free hand without looking at her and continued talking to Nathan. "Not every thing you see in the movies is correct about prison. A lot has to do with how you carry yourself. You have to be cautious at all times, but some of the horror stories you hear about in prison were not my experience."

"The hardest part for me was the aloneness. You were rarely alone, except in your cell at night, but it was always lonely. Being detached from everyone was a survival skill. If you were detached, then no one could hurt you, hurt you emotionally."

"My counselor had a real problem with that, especially for people in treatment in prison. She told me once that she thought the department of corrections could teach inmates job skills, and give them knowledge about self-help and recovery, but if men did not learn to attach, to trust, to regain the human experience, then it would be hard to be successful in recovery or on the outside. You see, if there were attachments, even healthy friendships, they were discouraged. I can understand why, but it made prison a very lonely place."

"You talk about your counselor a lot, Nate," Katie said. "What was she like?"

"*You* ought to love her, Katie," he said. "She stayed on me every minute about what I had done to you. I thought I had done most of the work of recovery until I entered the last program after the Storm. That's when I met her. She talked more about you and the others we had hurt, than about us, the addicts. There were quite a few days when I barely made it from the treatment building back to my cell before I cried about the things she pointed out to me that I had done to you."

"I always thought I was just hurting myself, that I had that right. She taught me differently."

"She told me once that addicts keep themselves hidden deep within, protected and surrounded by the very drugs they use. When a person like you, Katie, tried to get inside, to understand, I lied about my feelings and then got angry with you that you did not understand. I wanted desperately for you to know me, know what I was feeling, to know how afraid I was in my addiction, but I hid it with the drugs."

"She did all kinds of things to help us access our feelings. She played music, read us a story about a little worm named Charlie who never got to be a butterfly because he chose to live in a brown bottle."

"Nathan, she read *The Little Engine That Could* and told us we could have a different life if we worked to change. She even taught us Shakespeare and I will always remember the line from Henry V, "There is none so vile that hath not noble luster in his heart.""

Nate looked toward the window where the rain continued. "Treatment was quite a journey," he said to his family. "It was raining just like this the day my counselor told me I needed to understand that I might never be able to get my family back. We were sitting in her office and she said, 'You need to understand, Katie may have gone on. Even if she has not, it will be very difficult to stay in recovery if she is not in recovery as well. You have to remember, Nate,' she said. 'You are worth little to yourself or anyone else if you can't stay sober. Staying sober must come first, even before your relationship with Katie.' It hurt so badly, Katie. I did not think I could stand it. But I knew she was right."

"I hope you understand what I am saying now because it does not mean I am minimizing my love for you. That day in my counselor's office, I really knew for the first time that I could have lost you forever; and I also knew if I had it would not make me use or drink again. I was so sad, so terribly sad, but I had learned by then to just sit with the emotion and be sad. I knew the sadness would pass at some point, and I just knew I would not get loaded because I could not make things work out between us."

"We are very lucky, aren't we, Nate," Katie said softly, "to be some of the few who are able to save our lives together."

"Yes, we are," Nate said.

Nathan looked from one parent to another. Neither was talking. They were just looking at each other. "I am going to call Mindy," he said, and shut the door on his way out of the room.

CHAPTER 29

Nate should have trusted his instincts and started Nathan on the mound. He had gone with Keith, for all the wrong reasons. He wanted to *look* like he was doing the right thing, rather than *do* what was right for the team. Nate would have to remember to talk with his sponsor about this defect in character, this need for approval. It seemed like such a small thing, but when you were an addict in recovery, small things became larger things that could get you high or drunk.

Keith was struggling. It was hot and the extra weight that he carried was tiring him out. He was getting wild and had walked two batters. The third had a full count and another walk would load the bases. The score was six to three and a grand slam would put them behind and lose the game. It was the bottom of the final inning.

"Nathan," Nate called. "Get warmed up."

Nathan did not have to be told twice. He wondered why his dad had not called him to the mound earlier or even started him. Keith was losing this ball game.

Keith started his wind up. Please throw a strike, Nate thought. Keith did not throw a strike or a ball. He hit the batter and loaded the bases. That was it, he was done.

Nathan stepped up. He looked cool and fresh and that is exactly how he performed. His wind up was smooth, fluid. The ball crossed the plate and the umpire yelled, "Strike One!"

He followed it with a pitch that was low and inside. The umpire called, "Ball!" But the batter had wanted to swing. He was a little spooked by the inside pitch. Nate wondered if Nathan had seen it. He had. The next pitch was low and inside, and fast. The batter swung.

"Strike Two!"

Nathan checked his base runners. They were aggressive. Nathan took his time. The batter pounded the plate. He was nervous. Nathan waited.

Then he let go of the ball. It was hard and fast and right up the middle. The batter swung, but not soon enough. The ball went almost straight up, but the catcher was ready. He stepped up toward the plate and caught the ball completing the final out.

The dugout emptied. Nathan's teammates were all over him. All of them, except for Keith. Keith stood to the side, hostile and alone.

CHAPTER 30

When Nathan woke that morning, he lay in bed thinking. Everything was going so well. He had never expected that he would be so happy this summer. Nathan realized that he had been worrying for a long time about what it would be like when his dad got out of prison. He certainly had not expected that it would be without problems.

Already his family was beginning to benefit from having two incomes. His dad had been able to get his driver's license and they had bought a small SUV. His mom drove it mostly, and Nate took her older car back and forth to his job, but when the family went somewhere together, they traveled in the newer vehicle.

His baseball team had won both games and was now waiting for the city tournament to start. His dad thought they had as good a chance as any to win the whole tournament. He and Nate had been going to as many of the future competition's games as they could schedule. It was so much fun to be at games with Nate. Nate was able to point out so many things about the batters that

Nathan had not observed. He had not expected to get a pitching coach when his dad returned.

The other kids seemed to like his dad too. That made Nathan feel really good. Everyone just accepted that Nate had been in jail and that he had learned what he needed to learn about his addiction. It had been nothing like Nathan had feared.

Of course his parents went each week to the meeting at the old church. His dad went every day, he told Nathan, to an AA/CA meeting at noon. It was held during his lunch hour and sometimes he went to another meeting at night. Nathan did not mind. Nate told him that is what he would have to do to stay sober. Nathan did not care what Nate had to do—as long as he did it.

His mother was different too. She was *good* different. She did not seem so uptight. She was less angry. Of course, with his dad working too, she was able to work fewer hours at the hospital and had more time to study for her anesthetist certification. She would complete it in the late fall.

His parents were discussing whether they should buy a house and move out of the old neighborhood. The idea of a new house excited Nathan, but he could not imagine going to a new school, or leaving his youth group at St. Anne's Church. Father Sean had really been around a lot when Nate first went to prison and Nathan loved him. He would really miss him if they left the neighborhood.

Today was going to be a fun day, Nathan thought as he was brushing his teeth. All the kids who would be in ninth grade next year were going to a registration day at the high school. It was a time when the school counselors would talk about the TOPS program. TOPS was a tuition program for deserving students, students who had good grades, took certain harder courses, and who made high scores on the ACT test given before college.

Nathan had good grades and he had been recommended for honors classes in high school, especially in mathematics and sciences. He was eager to hear what the counselors were recommending for his schedule for next year. He wondered if he had any classes with Mindy.

He had learned something else about his dad, another of those secrets that no one had ever told him about Nate. Sometimes it seemed that there were so many bad things about his dad's former life that no one had bothered telling him he had ever been any different. Nathan got his new knowledge when he asked his parents if they had taken the ACT in high school.

"We had to take it," Katie said. "We were both planning to go to college. Your father had to take it earlier than I did because he was an athlete and you have to make a certain minimum score to play in the National Collegiate Athletic Association. The scores were submitted to a clearinghouse for athletes."

"So, how did you do, Dad?" Nathan asked. "Did you have to take it more than once?"

"No, just once," Nate said.

"What did you make?" Even Nathan knew that most college scholarships started at a score of 26 and you had to have some strong recommendations to accompany that score.

"I don't remember," Nate said.

"He made 31," Katie said. "I studied all the time and made 27, he made 31."

"Did you really, Dad?" Nathan asked. "You could have gotten an academic scholarship with that."

"Something like that," Nate said. Actually remembering how well he had done and thinking about his lost opportunities in sports made him sad. He had wasted so much. Every day, he was reminded of something else that his addiction had cost him.

So his dad had been a scholar and an athlete—that gave Nathan even more to strive toward. He was finding that more and more he wanted to be like his dad.

He got dressed and went into the kitchen.

"Are you sure that neither of us needs to go with you, Nathan?" Katie asked. "It seems odd to me that no parents are told to be there."

"It's high school, Katie. The letter said there would be a parent meeting later," Nate reminded her. "We can go then."

"OK," Katie said. She was dressed in her hospital uniform and was about to leave for work. She was going to be in the operating room for most of the day, she had told them. Nate had the day off. That was unusual, but some of the inspectors had gotten behind and they could not continue in their work until the inspections were complete. He was planning to paint the kitchen cabinets. They would be eating out tonight.

"Have a good day then, both of you," Katie said. She gave them both a quick kiss and was out the door.

Nathan followed soon after. He was meeting Mindy for the walk to school for the nine o'clock general meeting. After that, they would meet with advisors.

There were already a number of kids at the school when Mindy and Nathan arrived. Some were outside standing underneath the covered porch where buses unloaded and others were sitting in the multipurpose room inside. It was cooler in there.

There were a few teachers inside when Nathan and Mindy entered. Mindy recognized Ms. Sanders from a workshop at the library. She had taught a computer class there and since Mindy loved computers she had taken it. Ms. Sanders would be teaching mathematics and computer sciences in the high school.

They walked past the registration table and started to enter the large multipurpose room where signs gave directions to the different groups that would soon be forming. More kids were coming in now. The bleachers were filling up.

Nathan recognized Keith standing off to the side with a group of boys. They were laughing and Nathan could tell by their expressions it was at someone else's expense. When he and Mindy walked past, Keith spoke, loud enough to be heard by the kids, but not loud enough for the ears of the group of teachers standing nearby.

"There they go," Keith said. "The dope head's sister and the jailbird's son!"

It may have been the element of surprise, or it may have been the power of the punch, but Keith staggered backward when Nathan's right fist connected to his cheekbone just below his left eye. He swung at Nathan, but Nathan, quicker, ducked and Keith's hand hit the metal locker that stood behind where Mindy was now standing. Keith swore.

Nathan heard Mindy scream before he took advantage of Keith's distractions and lowered his head and tackled Keith straight on. Keith went down and Nathan was on top of him. It was Nathan's left hand that caused the blood to spurt from Keith's nose. Keith connected a punch to Nathan's eye that Nathan was too angry to even feel.

Nathan did feel the hands on his shoulders when the high school football coach literally threw him off Keith. The coach bent and picked Keith up off the floor and then, with a boy in each hand, hustled them both toward the administrative offices.

Nathan had never been in a fight before and he did not really know the routine, but he was certain that if this coach would let him go for just one minute, he would finish the job he had started. He was livid!

The coach slung Nathan toward a chair in the outer office and kept Keith in tow into the restroom nearby. When they came out, Keith was holding tissue to his still bleeding nose and the blood had been wiped from his bleeding hand. Nathan did not remember Keith hitting him, but he was aware that he had a puffy knot forming on his cheekbone.

Mr. Martin, the high school principal came out of his office. He looked very stern when he asked, "What started this?"

Neither boy spoke.

"Well?" Mr. Martin said again.

There was no way Nathan was going to tell this man who would be his school principal for the next four years that Keith had called his father a jailbird. He would rather get expelled and he was afraid that was exactly what was going to happen.

Keith spoke, "He called me a name."

Nathan could not believe it! He did not think he could get any more angry, but he felt his temperature go up even higher.

"Nathan?" Mr. Martin asked. Nathan was surprised that Mr. Martin knew his name. He did not know that high school principals, often former athletes themselves, were generally aware of what students would be wearing the sports uniforms in their high school years.

"That is *not* what happened," Nathan said.

"Do you want to tell me what happened?" Mr. Martin asked.

"No, sir, I don't want to tell you," Nathan lowered his head.

"Coach, do you think you could go out there and see if any students saw or heard what happened?" Mr. Martin asked.

"I don't have to. I saw and heard it myself," the coach said. "This kid with the bloody nose here called that—he pointed to the face on the other side of the glass window in the outer office—that little lady's brother a dope head and called Nathan's father a jailbird."

When the coach said "that little lady" Nathan looked up at the large glass windows. Mindy's face was plastered there and she was crying as if *she* had been in a fight. He looked away.

"Is that true?" Mr. Martin asked Nathan.

"Yes sir," Nathan admitted. He hung his head. Until now, Nathan had never felt ashamed of his father. He hated Keith for doing that.

"I need to know how to get in touch with your parents," Mr. Martin said. Keith gave him a number.

Oh how Nathan wished that his mother were not in the operating room working a surgical rotation this morning! He would so much have preferred to call her, rather than call Nate. She would see his bruises and feel sorry for him. Oh, she would probably punish him for fighting, but anything she might do was preferable to calling his father. He and his dad had been doing so well, but hadn't it been only a few days ago when his father had told him how he hated fighting. Nathan had no idea how Nate might react.

"The number?" Mr. Martin said.

Nathan felt sick. He gave him his home number. "My dad is at home," he said. "He's painting the kitchen."

CHAPTER 31

Nate had been mixing paint and he had a full paintbrush in his hand when he heard the phone ringing. He thought of letting it go to the machine, but thought that perhaps there had been some change at work and that he might be needed to go in later. He caught it on the fifth ring.

"Nate Matthews?" The voice on the other end of the line asked.

"Speaking," Nate said, using the end of his tee shirt to wipe paint from an arm.

"This is Allen Martin. I don't know if you remember me. You may remember my sister, Mary Ann . . ."

Nate could not imagine why Allen Martin was calling him. He had not seen or thought of him in fifteen years. He had been in school with Nate and it was true, Nate *did* remember his sister, Mary Ann. During one of the times when he and Katie had a break up in high school, Nate had dated Mary Ann briefly. It had caused him a lot of trouble with Katie. It had been trouble he had almost been unable to repair. Why was Allen Martin calling him?

"I remember you, Allen," he said. "How can I help you?"

Nate listened for a few minutes while Martin explained the events of the morning. He did not include what Keith had said to Nathan, thinking it better that he talk with Nate in person about that. "Is he hurt?" Nate asked. "Is either of them hurt?"

"They will be OK when the swelling goes down," Allen Martin said with a little humor, then, "No, nothing serious; I have seen worse. Nathan is in considerable better shape that Keith. You do need to come on to the school though."

"I am on my way," Nate said. He put the top on the can of paint, put the paint brush in a jar of water, scrubbed the water-based paint from his hands and pulled his stained shirt over his head.

Nate thought about leaving Katie a note, but decided that it might be better if he waited to tell her when he knew more. He was still slipping a clean shirt over his head as he walked out the door with his car keys in hand.

———————

Mr. Martin had placed him and Keith in two different small rooms in the office complex. It reminded Nathan of the interrogation rooms he saw on television detective programs. He sat and waited.

Nathan looked down at his hands. His right hand was swelling a bit, and he had a small scratch on his left. "Dad will probably have something to say about that," he said aloud to himself. What if he and Keith had both broken their hands? What would happen to the team?

Nathan was miserable. He was unaccustomed to being in trouble. Usually he was a student that teachers and coaches loved. What a bad way to start high school! He put his head in his hands and shut his eyes. One eye was beginning to hurt a bit.

Nathan did not see Mindy walk into the room, but he heard the door close. When he looked up, he was surprised to see her standing right beside him.

"How did you get in here?" he asked her, amazed.

"I told Mr. Martin that I needed to ask you how I was supposed to get home. You know Dad does not like for me to walk home alone. I just told him I had to see you a minute to find out what to do, that maybe I needed to call my dad."

"And he said OK?" Nathan asked, finding that hard to believe.

"He did," Mindy said. "He said to just take a few minutes."

"My dad is going to kill me," Nathan said, feeling even more miserable now that he had someone with whom he could share his feelings. "He hates fighting. He is going to kill me," Nathan repeated.

"I hope he does," Mindy said.

Nathan looked up in surprise. Mindy had never been critical of him. She rarely disagreed with him. He heard the anger in her voice and was distraught. "What?" he asked.

"I hope he *does* kill you," she repeated. "Fighting is so stupid. Did you think you were going to change his mind about what he thinks by hitting him? You could have just walked away and left it alone! You made it a lot worse. I am very mad at you!"

Mindy was mad at him—mad at *him*!

That settled it as far as Nathan was concerned—the whole world was mad at him. He thought he had been defending Mindy as well as himself and she definitely had not seen it that way. His hands hurt, the knot on his cheek throbbed, his eye felt funny, and Nate was on his way to school! His mother did not even know yet, but you could bet if this made Mindy mad, his mother was going to be worse. He wanted to disappear.

"Just leave then," he said to Mindy. "Just go . . ."

"I will," she said.

Nathan looked up at her. She was standing close beside him. When she looked down, she must have noticed his swelling hands for the first time. With her forefinger, she traced the swollen knuckle of his index finger. She took his hand in hers and turned it over, examining it for other bruises. She looked at his face and touched the swelling around his eye. He did not know it yet since he had no mirror, but his right eye was beginning to show quite a bit of swelling and turn blackish blue. Mindy continued to look at him with the strangest expression. It seemed that she had never seen him before. She studied his face.

Then she leaned over and kissed him gently on the mouth. Nathan was shocked. He had never kissed or been kissed before; and he doubted that Mindy had either. As soon as she kissed him, she turned and walked out without even looking back. The door closed behind her.

Nathan was left staring at the door. Not a single second had passed before Mr. Martin walked into the room followed by his father.

CHAPTER 32

Mr. Martin indicated a seat and Nate sat down across the small table from Nathan. Nathan looked up at his dad and Nate said simply, "What happened?" It was impossible to read Nate's emotions and Nathan was very uneasy.

Nathan looked to Mr. Martin for help, but Mr. Martin said, "Tell your father everything that happened this morning," so Nathan began. He told Nate about the walk to school, about entering the building with Mindy and was about to get into the part where Keith made the statements about Nate that caused the fight when they were interrupted. Mr. Martin was called from the room because Keith's mother had arrived.

Evidently, Allen Martin was comfortable with the manner in which Nathan was telling his father the facts, because he left to see Keith and his mother with instructions to Nathan to "tell your dad the rest."

Nathan went on. He told it exactly as it happened. He admitted to Nate that he did not remember getting hit in the eye or receiving some of the other licks. He told Nate the hits he remembered giving

Keith. The only thing he failed to tell Nate was what Keith had said about Nate being a jailbird. He told him about Keith calling Mindy's brother a dope head, but he left out the part about what Keith had said about Nate.

Nate listened attentively. He did not interrupt and he did not change expressions. "That's it?" Nate asked when Nathan was finally silent.

"Yes, sir," Nathan replied.

"You are sure?" Nate asked again. "That's the whole story?"

"Positive."

They sat there a moment in silence. Nate took Nathan's right hand in his own and used his fingertips to feel the small bones in the hand. "Squeeze my hand," he directed and Nathan did. Convinced that nothing was broken, Nate released Nathan's hand and touched the area around the swelling eye. Nathan winced at the touch and Nate dropped his hand.

"Could the two of you come into my office?" Mr. Martin said, holding the door open.

Nate followed Nathan into the room where Keith and his mother were already seated. Keith's nose had quit bleeding, his hand had a temporary gauze bandage and Keith's eye looked far worse than Nathan's. It was already completely shut.

A man Nate had never met stood in the corner behind Allen Martin's desk. Martin introduced him, "Nate Matthews, this is Coach Steve Connell. He will have both of these boys in the fall for football."

"Coach," Nate said, shaking his hand.

"I am very disappointed in both of you," Mr. Martin began. "You did not get started very well here where you'll be going to high school. If this had happened during the school year, you would both be suspended for three days. That would hurt you academically and it would suspend some playing time. But since this happened when we are not technically in school, I have a few more options. Coach Connell has asked that I turn the discipline for this over to him. He has a few extra things planned for the two of you after the regular team practice and he can always use some Saturday morning help in cleaning the equipment and the dressing room. If your parents agree to this, we can keep this incident off your record."

Nate nodded his agreement to the coach and principal. He realized what a break they were being given and he looked at Nathan to gauge whether he understood it in the same way. Nathan nodded.

"Keith told me what he said to cause the fight," Mrs. Arnold, his mother, said. "I think that your punishment is very fair, in fact, I think it is more than fair. Keith will be here, Coach, and he will do whatever you ask." She looked tired and a bit overwhelmed, but it appeared that, at least for now, she would be able to make Keith do as she asked.

"There's one more thing," she said. "Keith has something to say to Mr. Matthews." She turned to look at Keith.

Keith got up and walked over to where Nate was seated. Nate stood up. "Coach," he began, and he was interrupted by his own tears. He tried again, "I am really sorry I said what I did about you being a jailbird." He dropped his head in shame because he could not look Nate in the eyes. "Nathan was right to hit me," and he turned to Nathan, "I am sorry, Nathan."

Nate's eyes never left Keith's face and he said, "I accept your apology, Keith. What you said is true. I spent time in jail. I was away from Nathan and his mother for five years. Drugs and alcohol had been ruining my life. I hurt the people who loved me and I hurt myself. I was not allowing God to direct my life. I've paid for what I did wrong to society, now I am trying to pay for what I did wrong with my family and live my life the way that God intended."

Nate continued talking to Keith, "That time of being punished for what I did is over for me—now this is over. We are not going to keep thinking about it or worrying about it. Right now I want you to see if that hand needs some stitches and get it well before the tournament starts." Nate put his hand on Keith's shoulder and smiled to his mother. "Thank you," Nate said to her.

Just as quickly his smile faded as he looked at Nathan. Nathan looked away. "Mr. Martin, Coach Connell, Nathan and I have a few more things to talk about. Is it all right if we go home to do that?" Nate asked.

"Absolutely," Allen Martin said. He shook Nate's hand. Nate shook hands with Coach Connell as well. "Thank you, both," he said.

Mrs. Arnold and Keith left first; then Nate held the door open for Nathan and followed him out. Mindy was sitting on the bench outside the office. "Do you need to ride home with us, Mindy?" Nate asked.

"Yes, sir," she said. She did not even look at Nathan as they left the building and made their way to the car.

CHAPTER 33

Nathan could never have imagined a more miserable ride home. His father said nothing and appeared to be in deep thought. Mindy sat looking out the window and did not even glance his way. Nathan looked from one to the other and finally gave up and spent the remainder of the ride feeling fearful and miserable.

He was not afraid of his father in a physical sense. A glance at the knuckles on Nate's hands revealed tiny scars that were testimony that he *could*, and *had*, been physical with someone at some point in time. But he could never remember Nate even touching him in anger—ever! Still, Nathan had the feeling that an impending storm was forming and that he was going to suffer some damage.

Nate's thoughts were about treatment. His own recovery had followed the usual pattern. He had tried very hard to keep his emotions in check both in group and in individual sessions with counselors, but finally the dam had broken and he had experienced the healing wash of tears, and release. His counselor had explained that the drugs and alcohol had served the function of keeping emotions flat and that since they were taken away, it was normal to experience intense feeling.

Later during his time in prison, he had worked as a group facilitator, leading others who were in early recovery. Close association with the treatment staff had taught him to be aware when someone was slow to express extremes of emotion. "Just staying flat, with no real highs or lows, is not mentally healthy," his counselor had said. "People need to feel, and be able to express what they feel."

Nate was realizing how Nathan had managed to stay in the neutral zone of feeling for most of the time since he had been at home. Oh, there were exciting moments in sports, but sports were safe. Everyone was on the same team, wanted the same wins and losses. For everyone to have similar feelings about putting the family back together would be impossible.

He and Katie had experienced the full range of emotions, he realized. They had both laughed together and cried together since beginning to restore their own personal relationship and their relationship as Nathan's parents. They had discussed their anger and resolved issues that had been long-standing. Those had been private moments, moments between them as husband and wife. But, Nathan, Nathan had really expressed very little intense emotions about how he was feeling since Nate's return.

Nate realized all too well that some of Nathan's emotions had begun to be expressed the moment his fist struck Keith's face, but basically, Nathan was emotionally flat. Nate knew there was strong emotion there, likely anger at him for his years of incarceration. He knew also, that the sooner he was able to get Nathan to express that emotion and allow the flood of feeling that followed, the healthier

Nathan would be. As he turned the car into the parking space, he realized, he was going to have to make Nathan angry and he, too, dreaded what was about to come.

The apartment was quiet when they entered. Katie would be at work for several more hours, so he and Nathan would be alone. Nate offered a prayer of thankfulness that he had been at home today when Nathan had needed him. Nate had begun to notice the way in which his Higher Power took care of even the smallest details in his life.

Nathan entered first through the kitchen door and had managed to get a foot in the hallway on his way to the safety of his own room when he was stopped by his father's voice. "Have a seat," Nate said to Nathan, indicating the chair at the kitchen table. Nathan sat.

Nathan looked around the kitchen. The hardware on the cabinets had masking tape and plastic sheets covered the floor. Nate had been ready to paint when he had been called. His father was at the icemaker collecting cubes of ice, which he immediately crushed and placed in a small plastic bag. "Put this on your eye," he instructed. The bruise was developing into a real shiner and Katie was going to be very distraught when she saw it, Nate thought.

Nathan took the ice pack and held it to his eye. He still could not read Nate at all. Everything had gone well until Keith apologized, revealing Nathan's lie.

Nate sat down in the chair across from Nathan and looked at him for a full minute before he said, "I don't like it when you lie to me, even when you may do it to keep from hurting my feelings."

Nathan said nothing. He felt himself feeling angry and was not sure why.

"Did you hear me?" Nate asked. "You did not tell me everything and this is the same as a lie. I expect that to be the last time that ever happens!"

"I heard you," Nathan replied. "It will be."

"Do you have anything you want to say to me about jail, Nathan? Anything you want to ask about, anything you want to tell me about how you feel about it?"

"No, sir."

Nate allowed his voice to become a little louder. How he hated this, but Nathan had to know his own feelings to be able to deal with them and stay healthy. "I think you just told me another lie, son!"

Nate observed that Nathan was clenching his swollen fists. Still, Nathan said nothing.

"I think maybe you have a lot of things you'd like to say to me about my being in jail," Nate pushed harder.

"No . . . I'm OK." Nathan was struggling now.

Nate knew the routine. It was time to move in and force the emotion to the surface. He stood up and looked down at Nathan as he spoke even more harshly. "I think maybe there have been some times when you have been as angry at me as you were at Keith. I think that, son. Do you want to tell me I am wrong?"

Nathan was no emotional match for Nate. Already, he was starting to cry and he hated it! Crying meant weakness and he would not let himself appear weak before his father. He tried to stop, but his feelings overcame him and he felt vulnerable. His emotional self chose anger, rather than vulnerability. He stood up and flung the ice pack against the wall. It broke open and as water and ice cascaded to the floor, he faced his father.

"All right," Nathan cried. "All right, I *AM* mad at you. You stay gone for five years—five years! During that time I had to learn everything I needed to know from someone else. Mom can't throw a baseball—Father Sean taught me that! Mom doesn't know how to adjust the seat on my bike—I learned that on my own. I was seven! A kid needs a dad too, you know. What were you doing then, Dad? Where were you then?" Nate looked down at him without expression, knowing there was more, allowing him to continue.

"I was expecting a criminal to return. I was prepared for you to be wearing stripes and hanging out with the guys on the corner, but no, you came back a good guy. Then I started hearing about how wonderful you had been on the mound—that you gave up scholarships to LSU and ULM—Do you know, Dad, how bad I'd like to have that chance? And, oh yeah, you made a freaking 31 on the ACT test. I thought you were a criminal, not superman!"

I *DO* need to ask you a few things. I need to know *why*, Dad. I need to know *why* you threw it all away. What did you find out there that was better than baseball? Or Mom? Or me? Why didn't I matter enough to make you stop—why didn't you want *me*?"

Nathan was sobbing uncontrollably now. He had gotten up to stand up to Nate as he asked the hard questions. Nathan's eyes were red and he was sobbing every time he tried to speak. Nate reached for him and held him tightly to his chest, just as he had when he first came home. Nathan allowed this and clung to his father. This time the tears could not be stopped. Nathan continued to cry and Nate continued to hold him close. He wanted to shed tears of his own. No words ever spoken by a judge, or blows ever rendered by an enemy in the street had ever convicted or hurt him the way Nathan's words had. Nate hurt too, but this was Nathan's time for healing. This time Nate had to stay strong. He was father to this boy and Nathan needed his strength. He had to have it.

Nate held him until Nathan was cried out and then he said softly, "It was never about not wanting you, or your mother. It was never even about not wanting college or a career in the pros. Son, I think it is time I tell you my story."

CHAPTER 34

Nate moved into the den to wait for Nathan to join him. Nathan was cleaning up the spilled water and ice that he had batted onto the wall during his angry outburst. Nate had simply handed him a dish towel and said, "You clean up the messes you make in life, son, if you can." Nathan had gotten started.

Nate sat down on the sofa, grateful for a moment to think before he shared the events of his addiction and recovery with Nathan. What would he say? How could anyone really explain addiction to someone who was not an addict? How could he put it in a way that a child Nathan's age could understand? He had both dreaded and prayed for the opportunity of this moment since he had experienced the Spiritual Awakening that supported his recovery. Nate needed Nathan to understand. He needed Nathan to understand and not repeat the patterns of addictions that had plagued his family for generations.

Nate thought of the many times and places he had rehearsed the upcoming conversation. In the trauma of his arrest, as he had sat bleeding in the back of the police car, still under the influence of the drug that owned him, he had an awareness, that if he survived what was coming, the day would arrive when he owed his son an explanation.

Many times, he had been prayerful about Nathan. In the treatment rooms, Nate had prayed that Nathan would gain a knowledge of drugs and alcohol that would support decisions not to even experiment. On the weight bench, as he pushed his own physical limits, he had prayed that Nathan would develop strong physically without the lure of steroids. In the dining hall, he had prayed that Nathan's physical needs would be provided. In the line, standing and waiting, for his number to be called in the morning count, Nate had prayed for order in Nathan's life. When he received directions from a guard with only a fraction of his understanding of the recovery experience, he had prayed that Nathan would learn when to submit to authority and when to stand against it. And finally, in the absolute solitude of his cell, in the still, dark hours of the night, Nate had prayed that Nathan would seek and find his own purpose and relationship with God. He had prayed that in that relationship, Nathan would find the capacity to forgive him.

Seeing fathers and sons during family visitations to prison, Nate had experienced an unparalleled loneliness. Visitation had not happened for Nate after he had been moved to the northernmost part of the state after the Storm. Things had been too unstable between Katie and himself to merit the long drives from New Orleans. They were unsure what they could reasonably expect in their personal lives and for most of the time, it seemed the marriage had suffered irrefutable damage. As letters and cards became rare, rather than usual, Nate began to wonder if he would ever have a restored relationship with his son. Why subject Nathan to visits or phone conversations that would only cause him pain? His father was gone from him in these years. Little contact would be less painful. It was one thing he and Katie had agreed upon.

Only the visits from Father Sean had given him information about his family. The faithful family priest had managed to see Nate a few times each year, never promising an outcome, but assuring Nate he would continue in his prayers for the restoration of his family. Father Sean had been delighted when he realized that Nate had truly experienced God. The priest could sense the differences in Nate. The two men had developed a deep friendship that went beyond that of spiritual advisor and parishioner.

Nate had thought of Nathan and Katie almost every waking hour—and they had visited him in his dreams. Every thing he did, every hurdle he crossed in the regaining himself, made him more aware of what his choices had done to his family. Nate did not know that such pain and regret could exist in the human spirit. Counselors helped, but even the best could not promise that recovery meant being able to regain what he had lost, or more accurately, what he had thrown away.

When it had become almost unbearable, Father Sean had suggested surrendering his family to God; and Nate had done just that. "I give to You what You gave to me. Keep them safe," he had prayed.

And so, Nate had gone on, serving every day of his five-year sentence, growing, learning, working his recovery program. It had not always been easy, in fact, it was hardly ever easy. Daily, he had become more healthy spiritually, mentally, and physically. Nate had done the best he could, one day at a time, and now the day was here. The day was here to tell his son how it all had happened.

He offered one last prayer, "Give me the right words. I don't want Nathan to ever suffer as I have. Use me, if You need, to bring Nathan close to You. If I have to suffer more, let me suffer more, but now, it is about Nathan."

Just as Nate completed his prayer, Nathan came into the room.

"OK, Dad," Nathan said patiently. "Tell me your story."

CHAPTER 35

"You never knew your grandfather, my father," Nate began. "He died before you were born. Cigarettes and alcohol are a bad combination. He had lung cancer and he died the summer between my junior and senior year. He was a veteran of the Viet Nam War and he was filled with anger. When he drank, which was every day, he came home and started an argument with my mother. If she responded in a way he did not like, he hit her. He hit her a lot."

You know I am an only child. When I was young, I used to hide in my room when he hit her. As I got older, I tried to stop it. That usually did not go well for me. In fact, family services almost took me from the home at one time. My dad told me I had better convince the case worker that our home was fine if I knew what was best for me and my mom. I lied about how he was hurting us, and I stayed with my family.

It made me mad at my mother that she would never leave. I thought our lives would be fine if she would leave him. I know now that she could not. She was co-dependent with my father. That means that she felt it was her job to take care of him. My mother thought a wife's job was to stay with her husband, no matter what. Her own father, my grandfather had been an alcoholic.

I hope you are paying attention, Nathan, to the number of people in your family that were alcoholics or addicts. It is very important that you understand that.

Anyway, as I got older, near your age now, I started staying away from home as much as I could. I didn't want anyone to know what was happening at my house. I did not know it was a disease, I just thought my dad was mean. I was ashamed of him. There were times when I thought I hated him.

He needed mental health counseling, treatment. Who knows what he had experienced in the war that he wanted to forget, but I did not understand any of that. I just knew I didn't want to be there.

The guys I ran with drank beer. I did, too. I started playing baseball in the summer leagues. The coach at the high school saw me play and he visited my dad and told him that he wanted me to play in high school. Dad was all for that, but he never came to a single game. Before Mom died, she told me she thought he had known I would be embarrassed, so he stayed at home. Was that supposed to make me feel good?"

Nate looked away. He was quiet for a minute and Nathan thought he might be stopping, but Nate continued. "So I played ball, drank some with the guys and tried to hide it from the coach. It was what everybody was doing. But not everybody was loaded genetically the way I was."

"Your mom and I dated throughout high school. She knew I would drink some times and she hated it. It wasn't that she hated drinking. She hated *me* drinking. She said it made me act different. Sometimes we would fight when I had a few beers. I did not think the fights had anything to do with drinking. I just thought she was trying to tell me what to do."

I was smoking weed by my senior year. There was not much drug testing of athletes back then, so I could get away with it. I did OK during ball season, but when baseball was over, for me, the party was on. I can see now that when I had baseball, my self-esteem was better. Without baseball, I thought I was nothing. Drinking made me feel like a part of the group.

Katie hated it more and more. I hid it more and more. In the fall of my senior year, we broke up. Your mother was an old-fashioned girl and she wasn't into the kind of relationship I wanted at that time. When she would not change, I found a girl who would—a party girl. (Nate did not tell Nathan that 'party girl' had been Mary Ann Martin, sister of Allen Martin. Some things needed to remain private.)

Katie was angry and heartbroken and it was 100% my fault. She knew exactly what was going on with me and Mary Ann. Katie got plenty of offers for dates, but she wouldn't even go out with anyone else. She lost weight, her grades suffered.

I had exactly what I wanted. The girl I cared about was at home pining for me and I was with another 'doing me'! I was really selfish and misguided. Father Sean was the new, young priest at the church and he tried to talk with me, but it did no good.

By Christmas, I was getting sick of the girl I was dating and I wanted your mom back. When she finally agreed to go to the New Year's Dance with someone else, I couldn't stand it. I quit seeing anyone else and started trying to get her to forgive me. That started a pattern with us. I would do something stupid and then beg her to forgive me, take me back, and she would.

Getting her back was not hard. She loved me and I knew it. She refused to see me for a while, but finally did and we got back together. Baseball season was coming. Your mom and I were a couple again and everything was OK. I had even slowed down my drinking then in an effort to show your mom that I was serious about our relationship. I still smoked weed, though, and she did not know."

Nate stopped talking again for a moment. It seemed as if he were gathering his thoughts and deciding how much he should tell Nathan. Nathan looked at him with expectation, "What?" he asked.

Nate continued. He would tell him the truth, he decided. "I was a very selfish eighteen-year-old idiot," Nate said. He looked out the window, and seemed almost to be talking to himself. "Katie was so in love with me, so glad that we were back together. She had been threatened by my dating someone else and hurt by my relationship with the other girl. I took advantage of that. I took our relationship to places that Katie was not ready to go. I manipulated her and used my greater knowledge of sexual feelings. I told her not to worry, that I knew how to be safe, that nothing would happen. I abused her feelings for me."

Then Nate seemed to remember that there was someone else in the room. He looked back at Nathan. "Do you understand what I mean, son?"

"I think I do, Dad. I think you are about to tell me how I came into being. I know how old I am and I know how old you are. I can subtract," Nathan said. "I had pretty well figured out this part already."

"Sex is a wonderful thing between a man and woman who love each other and who are old enough for the responsibility. Your mother and I loved each other, but the responsibility was not something I even considered. Katie told me she was pregnant the day before the season opener—100% my fault again!

"We went to Father Sean. He was a young priest then, just assigned to St. Anne's. He went with us to tell her parents. It was awful for Katie. We wanted you, please, don't ever think we did not want you," Nate assured Nathan, "but I had just not acted like a man. A man considers the woman he loves. I had not considered Katie. I was still 'doing me,' and at the time the consequences had not mattered. Everything I did seemed to make me feel worse about myself."

"We got married, a small ceremony in the chapel at St. Anne's. Nana and Pop helped us get an apartment. College offers were coming in from all over. The only two I really considered were LSU and ULM. My mother died that spring. She had pneumonia. I didn't think anyone died of pneumonia any more. After my dad died, she only lived eleven more months. It was like she was lost without him. She just got sick and gave up. I still don't understand it."

"Well, that made your mom and me want to stay in south Louisiana, near her parents. We knew we were going to need some help in taking care of you if we both went to school. I signed with LSU."

"We finished our spring high school season by taking state. I celebrated by getting really drunk and high with some of the team. It was the first bad argument your mom and I had after we were married."

"Colleges were starting to drug test then. I was tested before I signed, but pretty well forgot about it that summer. I knew I could quit the drugs before the season started. I continued to drink and smoke weed throughout the summer. I tried some ecstasy pills and a few other things that Katie never knew about," Nate looked away again. "Or at least I never thought she knew."

"Father Sean knew exactly what was going on. He kept coming by, asking us to come to church or get involved with some of the young couples at church. Katie wanted to go, but I was always too busy. Our spiritual lives were put on hold, and that was really crazy thinking considering we were about to be blessed with a healthy child."

"The fall drug testing really surprised me. Why were they testing baseball players during football season? I failed—positive for weed and ecstasy. I was put on probation for spring play, told I would be tested again. I didn't care. Nobody was going to tell me what to do, not even LSU sports officials. I continued to use, they continued to test. I got caught again and they cut me from the team. They suggested that I go to rehab—I laughed. I did not have a problem, I thought."

"Now I had a wife, a baby on the way, no job, no scholarship, no school. That was reason to use more. I started drinking really heavily and using whatever I could. I began selling drugs. At first, I just sold weed."

"Fortunately, I was completely sober when Katie went into labor. Nathan, your birth was one of the amazing moments of my life. I was there in the delivery room with your mother the whole time. When you were born and the doctor handed you to me, I have never had such a feeling. I loved you with my whole being, instantly! And, I have never loved your mother more than that moment."

"I stood there looking at you and I had such a wash of emotions. It seemed I felt everything someone could feel. I was overjoyed and yet, ashamed of my recent behavior. I started to cry, right there in the delivery room in front of the doctor and the nurses. I could not stop. I can still remember that feeling now. I know that God was dealing with me even then, wanting me to return to Him, wanting me to avoid all the suffering to come."

"I would not hear. As soon as your mother was sleeping in her room and you were settled in the hospital nursery, I left and got loaded. I had no idea how to handle my feelings. I was really in trouble."

"I first did cocaine the day you were five months old. After that, my own life was over. Cocaine is the devil's own drug—and there are plenty more just as appealing—and I became the devil's disciple. Every day I chased the high that I felt the first time I did the drug. Every day I woke up thinking about how I would get the money to do more of the drug."

"When I sold drugs, I told myself that I was doing it to support my family, but that was a lie. I was doing it to support my habit. Nana and Pop were supporting my family. I stole things from our house, from Nana and Pop's house, from the neighbors, from people I did not know. I did anything I could think of to get money for the drug."

"There were a few times when I tried to quit. I even went to Meetings on the street for a few times, but I never really worked the Program. I never really surrendered to my Higher Power. Oh,

I prayed. I prayed not to get caught. I prayed that Katie would not find out about my latest escapades. I even prayed for the drugs, promising that just one more time and then I would quit."

"I got into fights, got beaten up . . ."

"I remember that, Dad," Nathan said. "I remember when you came in all bloody one night and sent me back to bed. Do you remember?"

"Yes and no," Nate said. "I remember coming in after several beatings, but I do not remember your being up. I was having some blackouts then—periods of time I do not remember."

"I saw Mom get hurt one night too," Nathan said. "Do you remember that?"

"Of course," Nate said. "I am sorry you saw that. It had to be very scary for you. It was for me. I tried to stop after that, but I could not."

"I could not stop. I did that life for ten years. I was absolutely crazy. My life was truly unmanageable. I hated myself. Sometimes I hated your mother for believing in me, for believing that I could quit. I wanted to die, but I was afraid to kill myself, so I just went about doing it slowly with the drugs."

"So how did you quit, Dad?" Nathan's trusting face made Nate sad. His son still believed he had done something noble to stop his addiction.

"I got arrested and I surrendered," Nate said simply.

"You surrendered to the police?" Nathan asked.

"No," Nate remembered. "I did not surrender to the police, at least not too willingly." Without thinking, his hand touched a scar on the back of his head, remembering just how unwillingly he had 'surrendered.' "No, Nathan, I surrendered to God."

Nate continued. "When they put me into the back of the patrol car, I was relieved. I knew there were several warrants out on me and that they would know that in minutes when they ran my record. I knew I was going to be down for a while."

"Down?" Nathan asked.

"In jail, down," Nate said. "I was actually relieved. I thought, 'Thank, God, it is over.'"

"I closed my eyes right there, right there in the back of the patrol car. I remember that even with my eyes closed, I could still see the blue light flashing. I prayed then. I told God that I was surrendering to Him He could do whatever He wanted with me, but I was done trying myself. I had made such a mess of things. If my life stayed a mess, it was going to be His fault because I was not going to do anything unless I felt Him guiding me to do it. He could teach me what I needed to learn, send me where I needed to go, it was no longer my will, but His Will."

"What happened?"

"I spent three weeks in a holding cell in Orleans Parish. I spent it mostly sleeping, being hungry, letting the injuries I had gotten during my arrest heal, and getting the cocaine out of my system. They took me back to court. I was on probation for some earlier charges of "possession with intent to distribute cocaine." I had violated my probation. The judge gave me five years, without benefit of parole." Nate looked up at Nathan, "He could have given me thirty."

Nate continued, "Exactly five weeks after I turned my life over to God, I was put in a treatment program in New Orleans. It was for Department of Corrections offenders who were addicted. God had a plan for me and he was already beginning to work it.

"What about Mom?" Nathan asked.

"She came to see me a couple of times in the parish," Nate said. "She was heartsick. Your mother is just not the kind of woman who is designed to look at the father of her child behind bars. I knew it and she knew it. She sent some letters, a card from you at Father's Day when you were too young to send it yourself, but it seemed the marriage was going to be yet another victim of my stupidity and my addiction."

"How did you know about us, what happened to us—like during Katrina?" Nathan asked.

Nate had a far away look as the memories of Katrina flooded his mind. "Father Sean," he said, recovering. "Father Sean always stayed in touch with me. He is a great believer in marriage, you know. He always told me not to give up on Katie and he reminded me that you were my son, no matter what."

"Weren't you sad?" Nathan asked.

"Very, very sad for a long time," Nate replied honestly. "My counselors in the treatment program helped with that. They told me I could not do anything about my family where I was, that I needed to focus on myself and learning how to live sober. I talked with them about a lot of things—what it felt like to have been an abused child, how I felt when I saw my mother beaten. I talked about my parents' deaths, what it meant to lose baseball in my life. I shed a lot of tears, Nathan. I don't mind your knowing that. There is a time for tears."

"Did the other men in the prison know you could have played for LSU?" Nathan asked.

Nate smiled, "No, I did not want them to know. It really didn't matter anymore. All that mattered was following the directions of my Higher Power each day and learning to live sober . . . and of course, you and your mother mattered."

He continued, "I was a little hopeful when Father Sean told me that your mother had not moved on. He said that she was not dating anyone, just going to school. Father Sean was careful not to give me any false hope, but I knew he thought Katie was waiting until I got out to see what to do."

"I had to ask her to let me live with you for a while. I had to have an address. I know now that my Higher Power had blessings in store for me even then. Despite all of this, Nathan, I have been given far more that I deserve. Do you understand that?"

"I think so," Nathan said. "Is that all, Dad? Is that everything that happened?" Nathan was asking his father the same question he had been asked earlier in the day.

"That's pretty much it—except for what happened with Katrina, and I will tell you that later. But you have heard the important part. Life is all about surrendering to God and finding His purpose in your life and then doing it!"

"I don't know what to say, Dad," Nathan said honestly.

"Say that this pattern of addiction that has caused so much suffering in our family for generations will stop with me. Say you will never make the mistakes I made. Say that you understand that drinking a few cold ones with your friends can start you down the path that I took. If you became an addict, Nathan, and spend time in jail like me, I could not even visit you there because I am a convicted felon. Say you will never let what happened to me happen to you!"

"It stops with you, Dad," Nathan said, "I promise."

"And, Dad," Nathan continued, "I love you."

CHAPTER 36

Katie had been so eager to get to the hospital that day. Her first stop had been the laboratory and her suspicions were confirmed. A few days ago when Katie had suddenly burst into tears in the middle of laughter, she had known. That had only happened one time before—when she was pregnant with Nathan. It was very early, but the doctor of obstetrics had assured her. Katie Matthews was pregnant!

She could not wait to tell Nate. Actually, she was a little worried that it might be too much pressure for him now, but she forced that concern to the back of her mind. Things were so much better now. Katie thought he would be delighted.

She wanted to tell him and Nathan together. She knew that seemed a bit odd, not telling Nate first, but they were such a family now. Somehow it was what she wanted to do. She just had to decide how and when.

Katie felt really good when she left the hospital. She was a little more tired than usual after a long shift, but now she had four days off. Tomorrow night was the beginning of the city-wide tournament. She and Nate had promised to help Father Sean at the church tomorrow morning. Father Sean had planned a party for after the game—win or lose. He was going to hang paper lanterns in the courtyard of the church and cook hamburgers for the kids and their parents.

Katie smiled thinking about Father Sean. He was really not much older than she or Nate and he had been a good friend to them through the years. He was very happy that things seemed to be working out so well. She remembered one Christmas when Nate was away. He had been gone about two years, and she was so confused. The holidays had always been really hard for Katie. She had always worked hard to make it a festive, but holy, time for Nate. Father Sean had spoken to her as they were leaving midnight mass.

"Nate is a good man, Katie," he had said. "Don't give up on him. I really believe he will figure all this out. I hope you will think about giving him a chance." It had made her even sadder at the time. Most everyone else had stopped talking to her about Nate at all. It had been a very lonely Christmas.

Now that things seemed to be working out so well, with Nate working his recovery program and her working her own program in Al-Anon, she was especially grateful to Father Sean for continuing to believe in them.

She had a spring in her walk when she stepped out of the SUV and headed inside. She wondered if Nate had finished painting and was eager to see how the kitchen looked with the new colors. When she opened the door, she saw that the job was only just begun and she heard Nate and Nathan talking in the other room. They were laughing, but they got quiet as she entered.

"Oh my gosh," she said, moving toward Nathan when she saw his black eye. "What happened?"

"I had a fight at school," Nathan admitted, looking to Nate for support.

"He had a fight at school," Nate repeated. Then he gave Katie a look that said, "Leave it alone for now. I will tell you all about it later when we are alone."

Katie did not miss the look, but a million questions were filling her mind and she needed to ask them all. "Whom did he fight? Where? Was anyone else hurt? Why? Is he in trouble at school?" and a wealth of others. All of them were on the tip of her tongue and she was about to start asking them in sequence when she thought about her sponsor in Al-Anon, Ms. Ellen. Ms. Ellen had told her only yesterday when they had lunch in the hospital cafeteria, "You don't have to be so much in charge now, Katie. You have a husband, a husband in recovery. You never really had any control over Nate's addiction. Let him be an equal partner now. Now that he is in recovery, it is even more important that you learn to share responsibilities with him, especially parenting responsibilities. This may surprise you, but Nate may know a little bit more about being a twelve-year-old boy than you do. Relax a bit. Work your program."

Katie remembered the conversation so well now. She looked again at her husband and her son with the black eye. "OK," she said. "Nathan, I'm sure your dad has handled this already. It was good he was at home today."

Nate and Nathan looked at each other. Nate knew what was happening. Nathan did not. He could not believe that he had gotten off so easily with Katie. "Do you think she is all right?" he asked Nate when Katie disappeared into the bedroom to change out of her nursing uniform.

"I think she is great," Nate said. Then he laughed at Nathan. "You got off easy, didn't you?"

Katie came out of the bedroom with a smile of her own. She was dressed in jeans and had a pink tee-shirt tucked in with a belt around her slim waist. Her hair was in a pony tail with a large clip. She looked perfect, Nate thought. He had never seen her look more beautiful. She seemed to be glowing.

Something about Katie's look struck a familiar chord in Nate, but he could not pull it up. He had seen it before, somewhere, at some time.

"Where are we going to dinner?" Katie asked. "It needs to be somewhere special. We need to celebrate."

"What are we celebrating," Nathan asked, "my black eye?"

"Of course not. Celebrating fighting would not be setting a very good example for your little sister or brother," Katie said. Her eyes fell on Nate, wondering if he had made the connection.

Nate made the connection. He knew why Katie was glowing even before she had finished her sentence. He crossed the room and hugged her so tightly it lifted her feet from the floor. "Katie! Katie!, I am so happy. I wanted another child."

Nathan was stunned. Apparently his mother was going to have a baby and no one had even asked him! He did not know what to think, and then, then, he *did* know what to think. He crossed the room and joined his parents. Both Katie and Nate put their arms around him in a hug. Nathan realized that this was the kind of thing that happened in a family!

CHAPTER 37

Katie had not been able to help that morning at St. Anne's as planned. The hospital had called around eight, just when they were sitting down to breakfast, to ask if she could come in for a few hours. One of the nurses in emergency was ill. Katie had agreed, knowing that she would be at home again by mid-afternoon and would still have time for a nap before getting ready for the ball game.

Katie thought about last night. Nate had been ecstatic at her news. He told her later, after Nathan had gone to bed and they were talking alone, that he had wanted more children, but had been afraid to bring it up. He wondered if she had enough trust in him now to risk having his child. Katie had assured him that she was as happy as he and explained how she would still be able to complete her certification as a nurse anesthetist before staying home for a few months when the baby was born. Then, she said, her salary would be so much better that with both she and Nate working, she could work only a few days a week.

Nate had confided to Katie that he wanted to go back to school. He wanted to work in addictions as a licensed therapist, one with addiction experience himself. She supported that, and they had spent several hours discussing how they could balance their school and work schedules to take care of the new baby and continue to support Nathan's school and sports activities.

There were functioning like a family now—making decisions for the good of the family and for the good of their relationship. Nate knew this was a sign that they were truly recovering from the trauma of the addictive past. He did not fool himself. Nate knew that he would decide every day for the rest of his life if it would be a sober day, but he felt encouraged. Life was becoming good for them all.

Katie did not usually work emergency, so she was already busying herself locating supplies. She had never liked emergency work, not when Nate was on the street using. Back then, she had only been a practical nurse and her responsibilities were not so great as now, but she always had a fear that Nate would be brought into the emergency room when she was on duty. She imagined him beaten, or stabbed, or even shot. It had been an awful time and she was glad it was over. Now she could take an assignment like this without fear.

Nate was on a ladder wiring the courtyard for the lanterns Father Sean had bought for the party when he saw Mindy hurry in. She went straight to Nathan and pulled him aside. Nate continued to watch them from his perch above. Nathan was listening intently and Mindy was very agitated. Nate watched Nathan take her hand and pull her to the center of the courtyard where Nate was working.

"Dad," he called up to Nate. "Come down, quickly." Nate could tell something was wrong and hurried down the ladder just as Father Sean joined them.

"What's wrong?" Father Sean said. Mindy was crying very hard as she tried to tell the two adults her concerns. "It's Jake, my brother," she said. "I heard him on the phone. He was really upset. He was telling someone that he would get the money somehow. I could tell he was scared, but I heard him agree to meet somebody. I think Jake is going to get hurt," she said, crying harder.

"Where?" Nate demanded. "Where did he say he would meet them?" He took Mindy's upper arms in both of his hands and turned her to face him. "Think, Mindy, where did Jake say he was going?"

"I don't know, I don't remember," she said and cried even more.

Father Sean spoke gently, "Think hard, Mindy, where did he say he would meet them . . . it is very important!" Father Sean looked at Nate.

"He said something about the bridge . . . I remember him saying something about the bridge," she said.

"He's probably walking so it is likely the bridge at the end of the park. It is fairly secluded," Father Sean said to Nate.

The bridge in the park was very nearby—probably only a ten minute walk. Nate was already running when he crossed out of the churchyard onto the street. Father Sean, Mindy and Nathan followed close behind.

When Nate crossed the one-way street and onto the playground, he could see the silhouettes of two men standing underneath the bridge. They were smoking and appeared to be waiting for someone. He could tell by their size that neither was Jake. A glance to his right caught Jake in his field of vision. Jake was walking toward the bridge and at this rate, he was going to arrive before Nate could cross the open space of the playing field. Nate pushed himself to run even faster.

Jake and Nate arrived within moments of each other. Nate could scarcely speak from exertion.

Nate recognized one of the men, T.J., and was not surprised when he spoke, "Nate," he said, extending his hand. "It's been a long while. It is always good to see an old customer. Can I hook you up with your favorite?"

Nate did not shake hands. He looked at the man he did not know. Nate could tell he was high. It all made Nate sick. He hated the thought that he had ever been a part of this life.

"Your boy here is a little late on payment," T.J. said. "He must be like you, using more than he's selling."

Jake had not said a word. It was clear to Nate that Jake was early in this game. His lack of confidence was apparent. He had no idea what to expect. "I don't have the money," Jake finally said. "I can try to get it."

The dealer Nate did not know spoke, "*Try* don't get it man."

Nate saw the gun before Jake did and he dived, knocking Jake to the ground. The bullet entered his chest and tore through his torso on its way to his spine. Time seemed to stand still in the moments before Nate lost consciousness. In those moments, the scenes of his life passed before him. He saw his parents, his Katie at the time of Nathan's birth and again, last night, when she had told him about the new baby. He saw Nathan as an infant, a young child, and finally as he had looked yesterday when he had assured

Nate that the cycle of addiction would end with him. Nate had believed him . . . at least he had gotten that done. Nathan would never be an addict.

Nate thought again of the unborn child, of leaving Katie to do it all alone again. He thought of Nathan . . . Nathan. He thought he could hear Nathan calling out, "Dad!" The sunlight in the park was growing dim. The edges were darkening. Nate wanted to stay. He wanted to see what it was that was making Nathan call out to him, but the light behind him was so bright and warm, so comforting. Nate turned his eyes toward the source of light and moved toward the welcoming arms of his Saviour.

CHAPTER 38

Father Sean went down on his knees into the dirt and pool of blood that was already forming around Nate's body. He knelt at Nate's shoulders and used both hands to hold Nate's neck stable. Nathan arrived moments later and knelt beside him, still crying, "Dad! Dad!"

"Call 911," Father Sean yelled, and it was Mindy who turned and ran toward the already forming crowd that had come running from the church at the sound of gunfire. "Call 911," she repeated as she met the group coming across the playing field. Someone had a cell phone and almost immediately the sound of sirens could be heard in the distance.

A black and white New Orleans police car arrived first, followed shortly by an ambulance. Father Sean never let go of Nate's head, but his mouth was moving. When Mindy saw Nathan make the sign of the cross, she realized that Father Sean was speaking the words of the Last Rites for the Dying. Mindy went down on her knees beside Nathan.

The paramedics relieved Father Sean and placed Nate's body onto a back board that was used for possible spinal injuries. When Nate's body was loaded into the back of the ambulance, Father Sean, Nathan, and Mindy were left standing a little apart from the crowd. Both Nathan and Father Sean were covered with dirt and Nate's own blood.

Father Sean spoke first to Mindy. "Did you see which way Jake went?" he asked her.

"Toward the lake," she answered.

Father Sean looked toward the lake and then back at Nathan. Police officer Tim O'Shay was a member of St. Anne's parish and he knew Father Sean. He recognized the priest's dilemma—should he go to the hospital with Nathan or follow after Jake? Jake may still be in danger.

"Go ahead, Father," O'Shay said. "I'll take the boy to the hospital."

Mindy never left Nathan's side and they were hand in hand when they followed Officer O'Shay and climbed into the back of the police car. O'Shay pulled out onto the street, just behind the ambulance carrying Nate's body. "Where is your mother?" the officer asked Nathan.

Katie heard the dispatcher's voice on the radio at the desk. A gunshot wound was coming in. "Male, mid-thirties. Gunshot with possible damage to the heart or spine. Very critical."

Katie saw the attending physician hurry into the room as she moved toward the emergency entrance, waiting for the ambulance. Already she could hear the sound of sirens. It was a common sound in Katie's life. She looked around the room. They were ready.

The ambulance came into view, followed closely behind by a
New Orleans police car. Both pulled under the covering for the
emergency vehicles and stopped quickly allowing passengers to
come hurrying out. The paramedics moved quickly to the back
of the vehicle.

Katie saw Nathan first, covered with blood, and her first
thought was that he was injured. Then as her mind processed that
Nathan was walking, hurrying in fact to the back of the ambulance,
her thoughts fell into place. As the ambulance doors opened and
the attendants hurried to get the rolling stretcher from the back,
Katie could not deny her recognition of the body on the stretcher.
She started to scream and dropped unconscious to floor of the
emergency room. It took Nathan a moment to realize the screams
that he had heard were coming from his mother.

CHAPTER 39

The hallway doors to the emergency room burst open and Karen, another RN who was in the advanced anesthetist program with Katie ran into the room. She was there to replace Katie on the emergency team working over Nate. Karen barked orders to another nurse as she ran past Katie on the floor, "Get her up and out of here," and then just as quickly spoke to the group of medical professionals surrounding Nate's body. "Get a drug screen on him."

Nathan looked around the room in disbelief. Everyone was so busy that they seemed to have forgotten that he and Mindy were standing there. In his family, Nathan was the only one standing. His father's body lay still on the stretcher where the team was busy sticking him with needles and hooking him to machines. His mother lay unconscious on the floor. Knowing he was of no help to his father, Nathan recognized his responsibility and he moved toward his mother.

A practical nurse had come to her side and was preparing to awaken her with an ammonia capsule. Karen had broken free for a minute and spoke to the nurse. "She is going to need something to calm her. It is going to be a long night. Either way, it is going to be a long night."

"She is going to have a baby," Nathan heard himself say to Karen. "My mom is going to have a baby."

Karen looked at him in disbelief, having been Katie's friend for years and knowing all the difficulties that she and Nate had experienced in the past. She was surprised to learn that Katie was pregnant. She looked at Nathan again. "Call OB," she said to the nurse attending Katie. "See if she has a doctor there yet. If she doesn't, call Dr. Powell. We don't want her to lose this baby." And then, just as quickly as she had joined them, she returned to the team at Nate's side.

Now it was the attending physician that Nathan heard. "I think the heart's OK. Get him stable and upstairs for pictures. Call the neurosurgeon." The rolling bed from the ambulance that carried Nate's body was headed out of the room, with six of the medical staff surrounding it, holding fluids, and machines. Nathan watched as his father disappeared behind the doors.

Nathan did not know what to do. Officer O'Shay ushered him and Mindy into the waiting room outside the emergency room. "Why don't you wash up?" he said gently to Nathan.

Nathan looked at his hands. They were covered with blood. He would learn later that as Father Sean had held his father's head, he had placed his hands over the wound to his father's chest as if he could stop the flow of blood. He let the police office guide him into the men's room where he washed away his father's blood as best he could.

When he returned, his mother was sitting there next to Mindy. She looked pale and she was weeping, but she was conscious. As soon as Katie saw Nathan, she ran to enfold him in her arms. "What happened?" she asked.

Nathan told her what he knew. People were coming into the waiting room now. Other nurses who were Katie's friends came in, giving her a hug and standing silently nearby, knowing there was nothing they could do or say to make her feel better. Tim O'Shay, true to his promise to Father Sean, stood nearby.

Time seemed to stand still. When the wait seemed near impossible, a young doctor in hospital scrubs appeared at the door. Katie recognized him as the resident neurosurgeon. He indicated a small room with only four chairs and Katie and Nathan followed him inside.

"Katie," he said, using her first name because he knew her and had worked with her in the traumatic brain injury unit.

"Our son, Nathan," Katie said, explaining his presence.

The neurosurgeon began. "He is alive. He is *very* critical. The bullet missed his heart, but lodged in his spine. It did extensive damage as it moved through the body. Right now, he has no movement of his arms, hands, or legs. We can operate, try to dislodge the bullet, allow the spine to heal. I won't mislead you—it is a very dangerous procedure. He may not survive it. However, he is generally in good health so his chances are better. Without the surgery, he is a quadriplegic, with it, he could have a complete recovery—or we could lose him in surgery. He has not regained consciousness. The decision is yours."

Katie stood and took a step back from the table, away from the doctor who was speaking. For a minute, Nathan thought she was going to faint again. She steadied herself by holding onto the back of the chair. Both Nathan and the doctor waited for her to speak. She did not.

Nathan turned to the doctor. "Operate," he said. "Dad would want the surgery."

The doctor looked at Katie, waiting. A twelve-year-old could not give permissions for surgery, but it appeared that Nathan had done just that.

"Operate," she said.

CHAPTER 40

When Katie and Nathan returned to the waiting room, Dennis Thomas, Mindy's father was waiting. He stood when they entered and walked right up to Katie. "Katie, I am so sorry. Nate saved Jake's life . . . how can I ever than you, I mean how can I ever thank *him* for that?"

He continued, "I have made such a mess of this parenting thing since my wife died. I've tried, but somehow I just can't seem to do it right. You know, though, what it is like to be a single parent, having to work, needing to be at home. I plan to try to do things better," he said as he looked down at Mindy.

"Thank you for your kind words," Katie said. "But understand— what Nate did—it is just who he is, who he is *now*." And then she thought a minute and added, "No, it is who he has always been. It is just that for a while the addiction kept him and others from seeing the real man inside."

Father Sean entered just then and he had Jake with him. It was clear that Jake had been crying and was scared to death. When he saw Nathan and his mother, he started to cry again. "Ms. Matthews, I am so sorry . . . Mr. Matthews took that bullet for me. They were going to kill me."

Then he spoke to Nathan, "I am so sorry, man. I . . . I just hope he will be OK." He saw his father then. Dennis Thomas moved to Jake's side and put an arm around his shoulder. "Dad," Nathan heard him say. "Dad, Mindy." Then the little family stood together and Nathan watched them, trying not to feel jealous and trying to keep his emotions in check.

Father Sean handed Nathan a bag. "I stopped by your house and picked up these clothes. Don't you want to get changed?" Nathan looked down at his shirt. Although his hands and arms were clean, his shirt was still stained with blood. He reached for the bag and disappeared into the men's room.

Dennis Thomas and Jake walked over and began to talk with Officer O'Shay. It was clear that Jake was trying to be cooperative with whatever the police officer was asking. They made an appointment to talk at headquarters in the morning.

Time moved so slowly, yet every minute that passed meant no bad news. Nate was at least holding on. At four P.M., Karen, dressed in scrubs from the operating room, came through the doors to give Katie a progress report. "They have located the bullet. It was just like they thought. There is a lot of repair work to be done. We will keep you posted."

Hours passed. Sometime around dark, Mindy handed Nathan an Express Meal from the McDonald's in the lobby. Although he had not eaten since he had breakfast with his parents, he really did not feel like eating now, but Father Sean said he needed to eat so he ate. Nathan looked again at the clock on the wall. This time it said 7:15 PM. The game would be underway—he guessed that Keith would be on the mound.

He spoke to Father Sean, "I hope the team does OK tonight," he said.

"Come with me," the priest said. He walked with Nathan to the area near the elevators. There was an overlook, a place where one could stand and see down into the lower lobby. When Nathan looked down below, he could hardly believe what he saw. Both teams, his own and their opponent, were there below. They were in their uniforms, their coaches were in their uniforms and they were sitting or standing quietly. In fact, no one was talking.

"Everyone really respects your dad," Father Sean explained.

"Thanks," was all that Nathan could manage.

About an hour later, Dr. Lee, the neurosurgeon, appeared in the waiting room. Katie, Nathan, and Father Sean got up immediately to go with him into one of the private consultation rooms.

"He came through the surgery OK. There were a couple of times when we were worried, but we were able to get done what we needed to do and now he is stable. If he makes it through the next six hours, he will likely survive. As for the movement, we will have to wait and see."

"Is it likely that if he survives and moves, he will still have some impairments?" Katie asked. She sounded like a nurse again, thought Nathan.

"Actually, not likely," Dr. Lee said. "I think this is going to be all or nothing. Any movement he demonstrates will tell us we have been totally successful. Now," he looked at Father Sean, "now it is up to Someone bigger than us." Father Sean nodded his understanding.

CHAPTER 41

Around 11:30 PM Nathan became observably restless. Nathan, Dennis Thomas and Jake, and Father Sean were the only ones who were not sleeping. Karen had come by to speak to Katie earlier and had brought with her some medication to help Katie relax and sleep a bit. "We will wake you if there is any change," Karen had assured her. "You know that."

Katie had told Father Sean about the baby. With that knowledge, he had insisted that she try to rest a bit. "One thing you can do for Nate, Katie, is deliver a healthy child," the priest had said. Katie had gone to sleep praying that Nate would be able to hold this baby, walk with it, just as he had with Nathan.

Even Mindy had fallen asleep, resting her head on her father's lap. Nathan looked at her there and realized he had never noticed how long her eyelashes were or how her hair curled a little around her face. Watching her there, he knew he wanted to talk care of Mindy, always keep her from harm. It was a line of thinking that was totally new to him and it was confusing.

Nathan got up and started pacing. Father Sean was watching him and sensed a much greater anxiety than he had observed earlier. "Nathan, come with me," he said.

Nathan followed him over to the landing and got into the elevator that Father Sean indicated. They rode in silence to the first floor. The hospital staff had insisted that the teams leave the lobby at 10:00 PM and promises had been made to call the coaches if there was a change in Nate's condition.

The lobby was empty and the hospital was quiet. The priest led Nathan through the lobby, past the reception desk and down a tiny hallway following a directional arrow that said simply, *Chapel.*

The priest pushed to door open and he and Nathan entered the tiny church within a hospital. The room was divided by a wide aisle. One side had a rather generic altar, with a large book on the altar table. The other side looked like the inside of any Catholic church that Nathan had ever seen. A crucifix hung on the wall at the back, a kneeling rail divided the altar from the set of ten church pews that faced it. An opposing wall held pictures of the Stations of the Cross.

Father Sean took a seat on the pew at the back and watched as Nathan walked slowly toward the altar. Nathan knelt deliberately, made the sign of the Cross, and bowed his head.

On the fourth floor alarms went off and staff on duty in the intensive care unit hurried toward Nate's room.

"Dear Jesus," Nathan prayed. "I have heard Father Sean say you hear us when we pray, and that you will never give people more than they can stand . . ."

Dr. Lee was awakened from sleep in the physicians' rest area when he heard the alarm. His normally steady walk turned to a run as he approached Nate's room. *"We are losing him,"* Karen said as he entered the room.

"...it's just, Jesus, I don't think I can stand to lose my dad now, not now when I have just begun to know him. Please, let us keep him for a while longer. I need him so much ..." Nathan stopped praying. He just stayed there at the altar on his knees. He stayed there on Holy Ground.

Dr. Lee felt Nate's pulse, hoping the machine was wrong. He ordered the injection be made ready. In fact, he prepared to administer it himself ... he looked at the clock.

CHAPTER 42

It was 6:30 AM and Katie, Nathan, and Father Sean were standing outside the intensive care room. Through the observation window, it was possible to tell that there was a patient in the bed, but the tubes and connections to monitors made it impossible to see much of the person. Dr. Lee was speaking.

"Things were very scary around midnight. We thought we were losing him. In fact, when I got to his room, his vital signs were dropping fast. Then, for some unknown reason, he suddenly seemed to take a turn for the better. He just turned around and he has been improving ever since," Dr. Lee said.

"Around midnight?" Nathan asked. Father Sean and Nathan exchanged a look, and then Nathan asked, "Can we see him?"

"You can go into the room one at a time," Dr. Lee said. "He still has not awakened from the medication we gave him after the surgery. You can go in for a minute, but he may not wake up."

"Is it OK to talk to him?" Nathan asked.

"Of course," the doctor said. "It may actually help for him to hear your voice."

"Has there been any movement?" Katie asked.

"None," Dr. Lee said. Katie knew that patients moved spontaneously after surgery, even when they were not awake. Father Sean put his hand on her shoulder. "Just have faith, Katie. We have come a long way on faith, haven't we?"

Katie tried to smile.

Nathan looked at his mother. "Can I go in?" he asked her. Katie nodded.

"Just don't be upset if he doesn't wake up yet," she said.

When Nathan entered the room, Katie and Father Sean stepped up to the observation glass. Nathan passed around the end of the bed to the other side of the room, putting him on his father's right and facing the observation window. He looked at his mother and Father Sean.

"Dad?" he said. Nathan stepped up to the bed and rested his own hand within inches of his father's hand. "Dad?" he said again.

Nate opened his eyes. He turned toward Nathan's voice. "Nathan . . ." he whispered.

Nathan looked up at his mother and Father Sean. Nate followed his gaze and turned his head allowing Kate and Father Sean to come into his field of vision. He tried to smile.

Nate looked back to Nathan and then down to his own hand, still resting inches from that of his son. Nate considered his hand. It was the hand that had been raised against his own father in defense of his mother, the hand that took Nathan from the doctor in the delivery room only moments after his birth, the hand that had held Katie's hand for what seemed like a life time, the hand that had hurled a baseball, paid a drug dealer, been confined in handcuffs. It was *his* hand and he willed it now to move. It dragged slowly, but surely across the sheet and grasped the hand of his only son.

"Dad?" Nathan said, realizing then that his dad was still there and that he was going to fully recover. Nathan knew he did not have to be a man yet. He could still look to his dad for the answers he did not yet have. "Dad, I need to talk with you when you feel better. I need to talk with you about a girl."

Read Part II of M-A's After the Storm trilogy as the reader

Follows Nate Matthews into middle recovery. See him as he struggles to learn that "meeting life on life's terms" is more than a recovery slogan . . .

Chapter 15

Jake Thomas leaned against the building and trusted the narrow awning to keep him dry. He was standing outside a neighborhood bar on Ninth Street. Forcing both hands into his pockets, he watched the drizzling rain. It was cold in New Orleans and that was adding to his anxiety -Jake Thomas was waiting.

Jake smiled, a smile that is more a grimace than an expression of joy. This reminded him of his earlier days of waiting for his drugs. It could be worse, he thought. He could be dealing with a slip of his own.

"Slip," Jake thought. "What a funny word to describe a return to drugs or alcohol. Slip almost sounded unintentional, and the return was never unintentional. A recovering person had to at least place him or herself in a slippery place, right?"

Jake realized his thinking was all over the place. "With reason," he thought, forgiving himself. He wished Nathan would hurry.

Jake had called Nathan about fifteen minutes ago. Nathan had Emma with him and had to drop her with Mindy before he joined Jake. The task before them was not one that could include Emma or Mindy.

Nathan pulled up in front of the bar and jumped quickly out of his truck. It was late December and already the extended portion of the cab of Nathan's truck was littered with baseball bats. Nathan was obsessed with baseball, but Jake knew that his mind was not on sports now.

"Where is he?" Nathan asked.

"Sitting in a booth near the back of the bar." Jake replied.

"Does he know you saw him?" Nathan's hand was already on the brass handles of the doorway entrance.

"Nope, I went in to buy matches," Jake said, a little apologetically. "I still haven't quit," he said indicating his cigarettes. "That is when I noticed him sitting there alone. He was smoking too. Do you have any idea what is wrong?"

"I have an idea," Nathan said. "Let's go."

The two boys, who were almost men, entered the bar walking with a purpose. Nathan led the way and stepped quickly past the tables where customers were sampling appetizers. Jake followed, dreading what he knew was ahead.

Jake stepped up beside Nathan just as Nathan stopped at the last table in the back. That corner of the room was dark and filled with cigarette smoke. Nathan looked down at his father. Nate was just crushing out a cigarette and reaching for the half empty long neck bottle of beer. The four bottles that lined the table convicted him.

Nate looked up slowly. "Hell," he thought. "Why did they have to find him here?" He was about to have to forge an explanation for his son and the younger addict in recovery that he sponsored. Nate was about to have to explain how he had lost his sobriety.

From – <u>After the Storm, </u> Part II

For the Reader:

M-A Aden and Nate Matthews are available for speaking and conference engagements. Contact us at our web sites for a complete list of activities connected with After the Storm, to visit our blog, and to receive notice of future publications. Watch for Into the Fog, a sequel to After the Storm, that follows Nate Matthews into the later stages of recovery.

www.afterthestormthebook.com
www.npss.vpweb.com